"Can I help you?"

Kirk grinned. "What did you have in mind?"

"I was thinking of a book."

"So was I, and all the titles have *love* in them," he crooned.

Tiffany bent forward to see what Kirk was reading. "Dorothy Sayers!" Her voice was full of pleased surprise.

"I've been trying to figure out what this Peter Wimsey has that I don't," he told her.

Tiffany put her head back and laughed.

"You're lovely when you do that," Kirk murmured. He cupped her shoulders with his hands and put his lips to hers, stroking them lightly, nibbling gently at the corners, tasting them. Ripples of delight, each one greater than the last, spread through her.

He lifted his lips slightly and whispered, "Just wait till tonight."

Dear Reader:

By now our new cover treatment—with larger art work—is familiar to you. But don't forget that, in a sense, our new cover reflects what's been happening *inside* SECOND CHANCE AT LOVE books. We're constantly striving to bring you fresh and original romances with unexpected twists and delightful surprises. We introduce promising new writers on a regular basis. And we aim for variety by publishing some romances that are funny, some that are poignant, some that are "traditional," and some that take an entirely new approach. SECOND CHANCE AT LOVE is constantly evolving to meet your need for "something new" in your romance reading.

At the same time, we *haven't* changed the successful editorial concept behind each SECOND CHANCE AT LOVE romance. We work hard to make sure every romance we publish is a satisfying read. And at SECOND CHANCE AT LOVE we've consistently maintained a reputation for being a line of the highest quality.

So, just like the new covers, SECOND CHANCE AT LOVE romances are satisfyingly familiar—yet excitingly different—and better than ever.

Happy reading,

Ellen Edwards

Ellen Edwards, Senior Editor
SECOND CHANCE AT LOVE
The Berkley Publishing Group
200 Madison Avenue
New York, N.Y. 10016

P.S. Do you receive our SECOND CHANCE AT LOVE and TO HAVE AND TO HOLD newsletter? If not, be sure to fill out the coupon in the back of this book, and we'll send you the newsletter free of charge four times a year.

Second Chance at Love®

BREAKFAST WITH TIFFANY

KATE NEVINS

SECOND CHANCE AT LOVE BOOK

Other Second Chance at Love books by
Kate Nevins

BREAKFAST WITH TIFFANY

First edition published September 1984

First printing

"Second Chance at Love" and the butterfly emblem are trademarks
belonging to Jove Publications, Inc.

Printed in the United States of America

Second Chance at Love books are published by
The Berkley Publishing Group
200 Madison Avenue, New York, NY 10016

BREAKFAST
WITH TIFFANY

Chapter 1

"LOOK WHAT JUST walked in!" Tiffany Bradford scowled and nudged Bennett Powell's tweed jacket. Once she was sure Bennett was looking at the man who had just entered the bookstore, Tiffany herself glanced away. Street people were unpredictable. This one might even become violent if he knew he was being stared at.

She began counting heads. Twenty-six people had come to The Red Herring to hear the young but well-known authority on Sherlock Holmes, Professor Bennett Powell, discourse on "Sherlock Holmes—How Well Did Doctor Watson Really Know Him?"

Nervous about speaking in public even briefly, Tiffany mentally ran through her introduction of Bennett yet again. She would begin: "Friends, Mystery Lovers, San Franciscans." This took in everybody: the dues-paying Followers of the Red Herring, the club devoted to detective fiction that met every month in Tiffany's mystery bookstore, other mystery buffs, and even—Tiffany's upper lip curled involuntarily—this throwback to the old Haight-Ashbury who was shuffling into the last row of folding chairs.

1

The Red Herring occupied the ground floor of a Victorian mansion that stood on a street between two neighborhoods. On the side that sloped toward the bay were trendy shops, little gourmet restaurants, and high-priced condos. On the other side, a scabrous patch of rooming houses and seedy bars dipped cityward. It was obvious which hill this latest arrival called home.

"What do you think he's doing here, Bennett?"

Tiffany surreptitiously returned her gaze to the man in the ragged leather jacket, torn jeans, and sandals. She figured his age as the early thirties, a few years older than her own twenty-seven, and his height, a little short of six feet. His build was compact and wiry. Long, straight brown hair streamed down from under a woolen knit watch cap. A dark stubble obliterated the planes of his face. Yet something about him belied his shabby appearance. Maybe it was his eyes. They were vibrant with interest—and they were taking in everything in the room.

"Perhaps he wandered in, thinking The Red Herring was a bar and grill." Bennett packed a lot into the smile he gave Tiffany. It was a signal that what he had said was humorous. It was also benign, affectionate, and maddeningly proprietary.

Tiffany smiled back automatically. Then she drew her feathery dark brows together in an anxious frown. "I've heard there have been burglaries in the neighborhood. He looks suspicious. Do you think I should call the police?"

Blond, linebacker-beefy Bennett Powell said judiciously, "No. If he causes any trouble, I'll handle him." He smiled reassuringly at Tiffany, and the flicker of worry left her wide-set brown eyes as quickly as a candle flame pinched out.

But glancing at the drifter again, Tiffany wondered if Bennett really could handle him. The man had a quick, tough look about him, an aura of power that, unleashed, could be dangerous. Yet in some ways, he didn't look at all like the bum his scruffy appearance suggested. There was too much energy coiled up within; too much steel in his gray eyes.

Bennett glanced at his watch. "It's time to start."

Tiffany stood up, took a deep breath, and from the front of the store faced her small audience squarely. Mercifully, her introduction was a short one. The clichés that Bennett himself had suggested rolled off her tongue: "founding father of the Followers"; "teacher of the popular course at Gifford Sage College, 'The Mystery Novel—Literature or Trash?'"

Gray eyes, with a hint of green in them now, partially hooded by sleepy, half-closed lids, prowled her body, making long, bold stops at her full-lipped mouth, at the soft curves that shaped her raspberry-sherbet sweater, and at the graceful, slender legs.

Tiffany's face flamed with mingled annoyance and embarrassment. She glared at the man who was making her lose her cool. He grinned back. *Did bums have chiclet-white teeth?*

Finally, thoroughly rattled, Tiffany wound up her introduction with a hurried, undignified, "And here's Bennett!" Then she sat down hard and audibly on the wooden seat.

Minutes later, she remembered the all-important announcement she had forgotten to make—a reminder of an author's autograph party set for the next day. She fumed with impotent rage. Admiration was one thing; insolent appraisal from a derelict was something else, especially when it flustered her mental processes and made her blood run fast, like mercury in her veins. And if she didn't know better, she'd say her reaction indicated she was sexually attracted to the man. But that, of course, was absurd. Her racing pulse was the result of fear, nothing else.

In self-defense, Tiffany opened her eyes wide to demonstrate rapt interest in Bennett's speech. She ostentatiously watched his mouth like a lipreader. But she didn't hear a word he said, and suddenly the speech was over. There was a flurry of applause, then Bennett was asking for questions from the audience.

Daphne Carrington, secretary of the Followers, got the ball rolling by asking Professor Powell if he thought Sherlock Holmes had ever been in love. Bennett thought yes, and advanced Irene Adler of *A Scandal in Bohemia* as his personal choice for the great detective's mate.

With a melting look at Tiffany, Bennett added, "Remember what Sherlock says of Irene?: 'She was a lovely woman, with a face that a man might die for.'"

"But how about Violet Hunter of *The Copper Beeches?*" Daphne objected. "Don't you think Sherlock's hobby of collecting violets showed a romantic interest in *her?*"

"No, I don't," Bennett said positively. "Not when you consider that every tenth woman in England at that time was named Violet."

More questions followed.

"What kind of violin did Sherlock Holmes play?"

Bennett answered swiftly, "A secondhand Stradivarius, which he bought in Tottenham Court Road."

"If Sherlock Holmes were alive today, would the crime rate be lower?"

The audience hooted with laughter at this ludicrous question, and Bennett smiled. Then his expression grew serious. "I'm sure every police force could use a detective with Sherlock's gifts of observation and logical deduction, and his talent for disguises."

Looking for timid questioners whose hands went up and down like jumping jacks before Bennett could see them, Tiffany glanced along the rows of folding chairs. Her gaze stopped at the bum. His eyes—a brilliant sapphire now—gleamed with laughter. A broad grin slashed white across his stubble-darkened face. In loyalty to Bennett, Tiffany tilted her chin haughtily and looked away.

She knew most of the people present, but there were newcomers, too. Among them were a rosy-faced priest, a lanky, look-alike couple who held hands and whispered to each other, and a Montgomery Street young tycoon in regulation three-piece dark pinstripe, a brown leather portfolio propped against his expensively shod ankle, and—incongruously—a gold ring set with three small diamonds on his left pinky.

Finally, Bennett was saying, "If there are no more questions, I'll turn the meeting back to Tiffany." On cue, Tiffany invited everyone to wine, coffee, and tea, and, as a special treat, genuine English trifle made by Daphne Carrington in honor of her countryman, Sherlock Holmes.

"And don't forget," Tiffany added, "The Red Herring is hosting a wine and cheese party tomorrow for Nick and Nancy Carroll, the famous husband and wife mystery authors. Nick and Nancy will be here from two to six to autograph their books and answer your questions about Farragut, their famous private eye."

The smooth surface of attentive faces broke up into individuals with different purposes. Some went to the books they had been eyeing longingly all evening. A knot of insatiables gathered around Bennett for more information about Sherlock Holmes and Dr. Watson. Others stood and chatted about the latest mysteries they had read and TV screenings of old favorites. A number went to the table where two jugs of wine—one white and one red—flanked a tower of styrofoam cups.

Only one person was at the coffee and dessert table. Tiffany's conscience smote her. The derelict hadn't caused any trouble. No one had objected to him. Instead of resenting him, she might have felt some compassion: He probably hadn't eaten for days. The proof was there right before her eyes. He was holding a plate of Daphne's trifle.

Impulsively, Tiffany went over to him. "There's plenty of trifle. And coffee and tea." Tiffany didn't think she should offer wine. Alcohol might be his problem.

"Coffee sounds good." The man took a styrofoam cup and held it under the spigot of the coffee urn. His hands were clean and his nails trimmed, Tiffany noticed. Then, as she watched, horrified, he plopped three plastic spoonfuls of sugar into the cup. *One* was not too unusual even in these health-conscious days, but *three?*

Suddenly curious to see how all that sugar looked, Tiffany peered down into the cup. He dipped the spoon into the black liquid and held it out to her. "Want a taste?" His voice was deep and resonant . . . and it shook a little with subdued laughter. Still, not wanting to hurt his feelings, Tiffany took the spoon and put it in her mouth.

She made a face. "Too sweet."

"Quick energy," he explained.

Quick energy for what? Tiffany wondered.

As he took a big slurp of coffee, Tiffany's glance fell on the gooey mixture of sherry-soaked cake, apricots, custard, and whipped cream on the paper plate in his hand, and she winced again. Suppose she were hungry and had nothing to eat but Daphne's trifle?

"Wait here," Tiffany said hurriedly. She made her way to her assistant, who was ringing up book sales. "Give me a fiver, Lois," she whispered.

Tiffany crumpled the bill in her hand and returned to the table that held the coffee urn and the big cut-glass bowl of trifle. The bum was still the only person there— Daphne's trifle had a certain notoriety. Tiffany squeezed the five-dollar bill into his hand. "Get a good meal," she whispered. She kept her eyes lowered so as not to hurt his pride. But when his hand closed over hers and he didn't say anything, she looked up.

His brilliant blue eyes sparkled with amusement. For a moment, she caught a glimpse of the kind of appealing man he might have been. Why, with a haircut, a shave, and different clothes, he would even look handsome.

Then Tiffany became aware that the warmth of his hand was permeating her skin. Moreover, its strong grip was exerting a strangely exciting power over her that didn't go with the handout she had just given him.

"May I have my hand back, please?"

He released her hand, but his eyes had that sleepy look in them again. Between narrowed lids, they now appeared, surprisingly, more emerald than sapphire.

"Thanks for the help, lady." His voice seemed husky with emotion—but what emotion, Tiffany didn't dare speculate. "I could use a good meal. I enjoyed the lecture, too. I sort of identify with Sherlock Holmes."

"Oh?" Tiffany wavered between staying and listening to his life story—didn't every down-and-outer have one?—and helping Lois at the cash register.

The drifter made the decision for her. He put down the plate of untouched trifle and his cup, smiled at her enigmatically, then turned and left just as a tide of coffee drinkers washed up at the table.

When the evening was over, the crowd gone, and only Daphne's trifle left, Bennett came over to Tiffany. "How do you think my speech went?"

"They loved it!"

"All except that bum, who kept laughing in all the wrong places. I should have thrown him out after all."

Tiffany nodded sympathetically, her attention elsewhere. Lois Weston was waving a good night. "Everything's done," she called out. There was a gay lilt in Lois's voice that Tiffany had never heard before. Usually, Lois was as impassive as a doll. In fact with her fortyish thickened waist, her doughy, expressionless face, and raisin-black eyes, Lois often reminded Tiffany of a yet-to-be-baked gingerbread lady.

"Thanks, Lois. Good night." Tiffany turned away from Lois, whose coy smile was for the couple she and Bennett made.

"I'll lock up for you, Tiffie," Bennett said. "Then what do you say we go out for some ice cream?"

"I don't think so, Bennett, thanks. I'm a little tired tonight."

"You look as fresh as though you'd just gotten up." Bennett reached for Tiffany, but she stepped back so that his kiss became a fatherly buss on the forehead.

He moved in for another try, but Tiffany stepped back even more decisively. "I really am tired," she said apologetically. "It's been a long day."

"All right, sweet, I understand," Bennett said with hearty cheerfulness. A few minutes later, he announced, "Everything's secured. The shades are down and the CLOSED sign is out. I'll just wait till you've got the cash in the safe, then I'll take off."

Tiffany removed the cash from the register, counted it quickly, and took it to the combination office and stockroom at the rear of the store. She twirled the combination lock on the squat little gray safe bolted to the floor and put the money inside.

"Thanks for waiting," Tiffany said to Bennett when she returned to the main part of the store. "And thanks for speaking to the group tonight," she added in a softer voice. "People never tire of hearing about Sherlock Holmes."

"You know you can always count on me, Tiffany." Bennett smiled benignly down at her. "And on Mother," he added thoughtfully. "She wanted me to ask you if you'd care to play bridge next Wednesday night."

Tiffany lowered her thick, dark lashes over the smile in her eyes. "May I let you know, Bennett?"

"Sure thing. I realize playing bridge isn't the most exciting way to spend an evening."

"What's the other choice—an orgy?" Tiffany asked mischievously.

A frown beetled Bennett's light brows. Then, obviously deciding to go along with the joke, he grinned. "Let's just call it a bridge orgy and not tell Mother."

Tiffany smiled sweetly. "Good night, Bennett."

When she had locked the door, Tiffany turned and looked at the room. It was a striking collage of grinning skulls, dangling nooses, smoking guns, bloody axes, and bottles of poison—the covers of the thrillers, mysteries, and romantic suspense novels she sold.

She knew every book there, Tiffany mused. She had ordered them all herself, had read most of them, and every month wrote summaries of their plots for *The Red Herring Reader,* a newsletter for regular customers. The store was her livelihood. It was also her joy and her haven, as she knew it was to many of the mystery buffs who had attended Bennett's lecture tonight.

Tiffany unlocked the door at the back of the store. This opened into the rear of the house, where she had closed off all the rooms with a view to expanding the bookstore some day. She now checked the locks on the rear street door, which she never used, the side door— her customary way of entering and leaving the house— and the door to the basement. Then she went upstairs to the modern apartment she had built for herself.

She raised the window in her bedroom and sniffed at the fog that wreathed the street lights outside. She listened to the mournful bleat of the foghorns out on the bay. Their melancholy music suited her mood. This was not a night to fend off Bennett Powell's vanilla kisses. It was a mysterious night, a delicious time to be in an old house that looked like the cover of a paperback gothic, to feel herself back in the foggy, gaslit London of Holmes and Dr. Watson.

Why not put herself there? Tiffany mused. She went to her bookcase and removed a heavy volume of the stories of Sherlock Holmes. Getting into bed and balancing the book on her stomach, she started to read, then broke off to stare at the opposite wall.

In her mind's eye, Tiffany saw the drifter she had given five dollars to. Hands in his pockets, his body tightly to himself, he was probably wandering around in the fog right now. What did he think of her? That she was good-hearted or that she was a sap? Or, Tiffany wondered, recalling the predatory green eyes with which he'd looked at her, was it neither of these two but something else?

A thrill ran up and down her spine. Then a piercing ache deep within her echoed the lonely wail of a foghorn. It had been two years since Owen was killed. The Red Herring and friends and dates with Bennett had kept her content. But contentment wasn't happiness.

Chapter 2

TIFFANY AWOKE TO sharply bright sunshine. A stiff morning breeze had blown the night's fog away and left the air brisk and pure. She washed quickly, pulled on a pair of gray sweat pants and a T-shirt that said "The Butler Did It," and left by the side door for her daily jogging.

Head up, hands chest-high, she ran by Wu's Dry Cleaners, Bud's Shoe Repair, and the mom-and-pop grocery now run by the original owners' son-in-law. Then, for variety, she left her street to run past the pricey condos and the row of shops and restaurants with names ending in *y*: the Greenery, the Eatery, the Pantry, the Bootery, and a fancy stationery store, La Papeterie.

Her face glowing, she let herself into the house again and sat down to a cup of coffee. When the doorbell rang at eight-thirty, an hour and a half from store-opening time, she was still in her jogging clothes.

The paper boy doing his monthly collecting, Tiffany decided, as she ran downstairs and flung open the door.

A man wearing a tweed blazer, blue button-down oxford shirt, burgundy tie, and amber-tinted sunglasses stood there. "Ms. Bradford?"

"Ye-es?" Tiffany drew her answer out in a long syllable.

"Do you always open the door like that?"

"I thought it was the paper boy. Is this a test to see how people open their doors?"

"Detective Sergeant Davis of the San Francisco P.D." He pulled a plastic card bearing a colored photo out of his pocket and held it up in front of her. Tiffany gave the picture a quick, perfunctory look and nodded. "I'm investigating some burglaries in the neighborhood. I'd like to ask you a few questions."

Tiffany smiled her approval. As the proprietor of a store and a home owner, she was all for vigilant police work. She opened the door wider and said, "Won't you come in?" She led the way up the stairs and into her living room. "Would you like some coffee?"

The sergeant stood looking around him. "This is nice."

"Thanks. The exterior of the house is great for a mystery bookstore, but I couldn't stand the wainscoting and dark walls that were here originally, so I had the whole room—paneling and walls—painted white and hung some David Hockney reproductions. Floor cushions and low tables," she continued, looking around, taking inventory. "And, oh, I streamlined the fireplace, too. The original mantel looked like something Pinocchio's father might have carved."

"Gepetto."

"Huh?"

"That was Pinocchio's father's name."

"I forgot." She shrugged. "When you don't have kids . . ."

"I don't have any, either. I'm not married. But I still remember Winnie-the-Pooh and Mr. Toad and Babar the Elephant."

"I'm strong on *Alice in Wonderland*," Tiffany said defensively. They both laughed then, openly, companionably. "Did you say you wanted coffee or not? I can't remember now."

"Please."

"Sugar? Cream?"

"Just sugar, please."

Tiffany left him still looking around at her living room, a pleased smile on his smoothly shaved, lean face. She returned with a tray holding two steaming mugs of coffee, white paper napkins, and a white china sugar bowl. She placed the tray on a low, square table and sat down on a plump lemon-yellow cushion in front of the table.

"I like to do this Japanese-style," she half-apologized, "but if you'd be more comfortable on the couch, please sit there."

"This is fine." He lowered himself onto a cushion beside hers and looked down at his legs. "What do I do with them?"

Tiffany stared blankly for a moment at the strong, muscular thighs stretched out beside hers on the celery-green carpeting. "You have to experiment with positions."

"I'll kneel," he said blandly with a humorous flaring of his nostrils.

Tiffany watched as he filled a spoon with sugar and tilted it into his coffee mug. He did this three times.

Was there something about sugar she didn't know? Was it considered good for you now? Or if Sergeant Davis took off his glasses, would he be . . . ?

"This room is rather dark. Are you sure you want to wear sunglasses?"

Grinning mischievously, he laid the amber-tinted glasses on the coffee table.

It was absolutely amazing! With hair the conventional length, stylish clothes, and a shave, he looked entirely different. Only his eyes—those mocking, now-blue eyes—were the same.

Tiffany felt unreasonably angry, put upon, fooled. Belligerently, she stuck out her hand, palm up. "You owe me five."

Eyes sparkling with laughter, he put his hand in his pocket and pulled out a bill. He put it in the palm of her hand and closed his own hand over it, holding it there.

Tiffany turned her head with annoyance. Really, she was in a bad way if a total stranger could make all the molecules in her body go zing and jump around, bumping into each other, just by holding her hand at nine in the morning. And nine at night, too, she reminded herself, hell-bent on honesty.

"Do you want your hand back?" he asked cheerfully.

"I could use it."

He let go. But as he did so, he trailed his fingers lightly across the underside of her wrist. She could feel their warmth on her pulse and was conscious of the quickened beat that followed.

This mere grazing of her bare skin had set up a delicious tingling that was making it difficult for her to look indignant. Nevertheless, she said bitterly, "You might have told me you were an undercover cop."

He smiled broadly. "I was so wrapped up in trifling with Daphne, I guess I forgot to."

Tiffany made a face. "Very funny. How did you manage to disguise yourself so well?"

"Elementary, my dear Ms. Bradford. I used a wig, a little stage makeup, and a few days' growth of beard. Now it's my turn." His vibrant cerulean-blue eyes took in the living room again. "How long have you lived in this house?"

"About a year. My parents bought the house several years ago as rental property, and I'm renting it from them."

"Do they live in San Francisco?"

"No longer. My mother has arthritis and needs a drier climate, so they moved to Modesto."

"And the bookstore—have you always been in that business?"

Tiffany shook her head. "I was widowed two years ago. For a year after, I was too stunned to do anything but continue in my job as a public-relations consultant. Then, when I was able to put my life together again, I decided I would do what I really wanted to. I've always been an avid mystery reader and used to dream of owning a mystery bookstore. The result—The Red Herring, a mystery bookstore."

"How's business?"

Tiffany tilted her hand back and forth. "It could be better, but I've been open barely a year. It takes time."

"I've got a couple of ideas." He looked at her with eyes now as softly green as molten emeralds. "Ways you could improve the store, I mean."

Tiffany inched sideways—away from the strong, sinewy thigh that was now touching hers. Sitting on the floor hadn't been such a good idea. Enough chemistry was passing between her and this Sergeant Davis to build an atom bomb.

Besides, why did his eyes change color like that? They were gray when he was the cold, analytical cop; blue to accompany his nice, easy grin; and green when he looked at her in ways that—Tiffany gulped and forced herself to be honest—ways that made her heart race and her nerves feel like conduits for long-forgotten sensations.

"That's very nice," she said flatly, discouragingly. "Did you say you wanted to question me about some burglaries?"

"Right," he murmured. "Have you noticed any suspicious characters in the neighborhood recently?"

"Only you," Tiffany said sweetly.

"I work best undercover." His grin was devastatingly wicked and totally male.

"Who's been robbed?" Tiffany asked coldly.

"Wu's Dry Cleaners . . ."

"Mr. Wu!" Tiffany interrupted. "I have a dress there."

"All the cat burglar took was some jade Mr. Wu kept in the store because he thought it was a safer place than his apartment."

"Cat burglar?" Tiffany repeated.

Sergeant Davis passed his hand wearily over his forehead. "We call him that because he gets in and out of places as easily as a cat. So far he's gotten away with every robbery he's pulled. He also hit Bud's Shoe Repair for the cash in the till and got a coin collection in a private home."

"But that's all small-time stuff, isn't it?"

"Right. However, it seems to show an inside knowledge of what's available in the neighborhood, and there are a lot of rich pickings on the next street if our boy gets cocky and decides to go for the gold."

"I'm sorry I can't help you," Tiffany said with sincerity. "I haven't noticed anything unusual around here."

"I didn't think you had."

Tiffany raised her soft, feathery eyebrows. "Then why are you here, Sergeant?"

He half-closed his eyes and grinned. "I'm interested in the lay of the land, so to speak—in who comes to your store." He looked around the room again. "And your house interests me, too. It's the only Victorian in the neighborhood."

"So?"

"So, if it's typical, it's honeycombed with small rooms and might even have a basement. Some of them do."

"This one does. But again, so what?"

Davis passed his hand over his forehead again, and Tiffany noticed the charcoal-gray smudges of fatigue under his eyes and the grooves that ran from the sharp blade of his nose to his mouth. "So far as we know, none of the loot has been fenced yet, so he must be stashing it somewhere."

"Well, he's not stashing it here," Tiffany said indignantly.

Davis shrugged. "It was just an idea. Do you have anything in your house or store that might interest him? He seems to be going for small items."

"My husband picked up some wood carvings when he was in Africa."

"I'd like to see them." He rose and, reaching his hands down to hers, pulled Tiffany to her feet. That left them standing close, holding hands again. "I appreciate your cooperation, Ms. Bradford."

She dropped her hands ostentatiously. "We don't want to obliterate the fingerprints, do we, Detective Davis?"

He grinned. "The name's Kirk, and so you don't feel funny using it, I'll call you Tiffany. May I see those African carvings now, Tiffany?"

"I'll bring them to you." Tiffany went into her bedroom and leaned her head for a moment against the cool glass of the window. Everything within her seemed to be overheated and in violent motion.

"Kirk Davis." She said his name out loud, trying to know him quickly, this man who, as a street person or policeman, tugged at her senses as no one had in a long time.

Conscious of a step behind her, she turned. Kirk was standing there, a quizzical look on his face.

"This is my bedroom!" Tiffany protested.

"I didn't think it was the kitchen." His voice was gentle, humorous. "You were gone so long, I began to worry about you."

Tiffany stared at him a moment, perplexed. *Worry* went beyond mere attraction. It was a caring emotion; something she hadn't expected from him. And why should Sergeant Davis be worried about her in her own home?

She turned abruptly and opened a bureau drawer. She took out a shoe box and removed a foot-high wooden figure from a bed of white cotton. The statuette had the head and horns of an antelope, a swanlike neck, and a pronounced ridge along its back. "This is a Chi-Wara, a mythical being that supposedly taught the Bambara people of Mali how to farm. I have another similar to this."

Kirk took the figurine from her and held it in his hand. "Is it valuable?"

"In the present art market, yes, but less so than the other one."

He handed it back. "Don't you have a more secure

place to keep these statues? You must have an office safe."

"I do; but because I live above the store, it's very important to me to keep my business and personal lives separate. Also, until now, there hasn't been any crime in the neighborhood." Tiffany shrugged. "Besides, nobody knows I have these little statues, and nothing about the house suggests affluence."

Tiffany put the Chi-Wara away, and they returned to the living room.

She stood by the coffee table, expecting him to leave, but he extended a hand toward the floor cushions and said, "I'd like to hear more about those carvings."

Was it against the law, Tiffany wondered, to refuse a police officer information? With studied casualness, she shrugged and sat down on the same lemon-yellow cushion, tucking her legs under her, schoolgirl fashion. Kirk sat next to her and took a long sip of his coffee.

"It must be cold. I'll get more."

He put his hand on her arm. "No, I like it this way." His eyes held hers in a humorous, knowing look.

Tiffany very deliberately took his hand and placed it on the table. "About those carvings—my husband, Owen, was a veterinarian, but before he started his practice— his dog and cat practice, he called it—he took time off to visit some of the wild game preserves in Africa. That's when he got the figurines we've been talking about."

"That's great!" Kirk said enthusiastically. "I've always been interested in big game myself. Did you go to Africa with him?"

Tiffany shook her head. "I didn't know him then. We met soon after he returned. I was doing public relations for the city zoo. Because of his African experience, Owen was called in frequently for consultation. We got married just after he started his practice, but he wasn't happy taking care of family pets. His heart was with big animals."

"I can relate to that."

"Soon after, he sold his practice and took a job with one of the private animal safaris in southern California. You know, the kind where people drive through with their windows closed to look at lions and tigers and elephants in what appears to be their natural environment."

Kirk nodded knowingly. "And how did that work out?"

"Some of the animals got into trouble there. An elephant knocked a trainer down and crushed him to death, and there were other incidents. Owen didn't think the animals had been handled right. So he followed them to a place way out in the boonies, sort of a reform school for bad characters, and worked at trying to rehabilitate them. He had a lot of success."

"Terrific!" Kirk breathed.

"Not so terrific," Tiffany said dryly. "He began to be almost obsessed with rescuing these animals. If there was any trouble with one of them, any danger, he told the other trainers to stay back. Then he went in and handled the creature. He kept reminding people that these animals were out of their natural environments." Tiffany's tone remained detached and objective, but her voice dropped lower. "The day before he was killed, he even said to me, 'Tiff, remember, if anything happens to me, it isn't the animal's fault.'"

Kirk let out a long, almost inaudible whistle. "How did it happen?" he asked tersely.

"A Siberian tiger with the cute name of Snowflake got loose. Owen told the others not to shoot and to stay back. He tried to stun her with a tranquilizer dart, but she got to him first."

Kirk put his hand over hers. It seemed to Tiffany that with his firm grip he was trying to press his strength into her. But she didn't need his support. She had completed the passages of widowhood, and she had done it using her own strength.

"It's all right," she said. "At first it was like being hit by a two-ton truck. About all I could do was put one foot in front of the other day after day till I thought the rest of my life would be like that. But it wasn't. I recovered, and it doesn't hurt any more."

Kirk studied her for a long moment, then stood up. Briskly, as though to overcome reluctance, he said, "I've got to get down to headquarters and make out some reports. I'm working overtime today."

"A policeman's lot is not a happy one," Tiffany remarked teasingly, standing too.

"You could make it a lot happier."

"I didn't tell you, but I'm not civic-minded."

"Have dinner with me tonight," Kirk coaxed.

"I don't think so."

"It would help my investigation."

Wide-eyed, Tiffany looked up at him. "Is this the way the police work?"

"On TV, no; in real life, if we're lucky. Make me lucky," he said huskily.

Tiffany threw her head back and laughed, her clear brown eyes sparkling like a fast-running brook.

"Sounds good," Kirk said with a smile. "The laugh, I mean. Want to go for broke tonight? A yuk a minute?"

"Won't you be on duty?"

"We'll eat unromantically early. Say, seven. All right?"

"Yes." Tiffany's heart began to beat fast at the prospect of a date with Kirk Davis.

"Tonight then," he said softly, looking into her eyes. Then, on what seemed to be impulse, he lowered his lips to hers. Their lips clung, each to each, like warm, ripe fruit. Hemmed in between the big cushions and the low table, their bodies touched.

Tiffany's blood began to heat. A tremor of desire passed through her. She put her hands up to Kirk's chest— but whether to draw him closer or push him away, she herself didn't know.

Then, slowly, reluctantly, he took his mouth away and walked to the door, moving gracefully on the balls of his feet.

Tiffany stood for a long time, staring unseeingly at a

bookcase against the wall. She touched her tongue to her lips, seeking to taste Kirk's kiss again, to hold it in her own sultry, excited mouth.

Then her eyes focused on a shelf of favorite books, the mystery novels of Dorothy Sayers. Had Harriet Vane felt this way when Lord Peter Wimsey kissed her? Not that there was any comparison between Lord Peter, the erudite, aristocratic amateur sleuth, and Kirk Davis, undercover city cop with a boxer's body and the aggressiveness to match.

Tiffany arched a speculative eyebrow. But hadn't Lord Peter come on strong to Harriet when she was accused of murder and he was the only one who could prove her innocence? Tiffany smiled. Maybe there wasn't that much difference between a policeman and a peer, after all. Besides, Lord Peter didn't have fascinating, color-coded eyes.

Chapter 3

TIFFANY WAS ALWAYS punctual in opening The Red Herring at ten o'clock on the dot and, if there were no customers in the store, closing it at six. Kirk's morning visit had put her behind, and she hurried now to shower and dress and grab a bite of breakfast.

But as she fluffed up her damp hair with a dryer, her eyes took on a dreamy look. With a little stretch of the imagination, she could feel Kirk's muscular thigh against hers. Her whole body seemed to shiver as she relived the suspense of wondering, as his eyes turned green, what he would do. Just thinking about Kirk caused a delicious rush of excitement inside her.

The hair dryer's thin whine made Tiffany almost miss the phone. The caller was her assistant, Lois Weston.

"Tiffany, I hate to tell you this, but I'm not coming in today. I've got a terrible sore throat."

Tiffany groaned inwardly. Lois had called in sick so often in the last few weeks that it didn't seem possible this latest illness could be genuine. Yet she hesitated to come right out and accuse her assistant of malingering.

"I'm sorry you're not feeling up to par, Lois, but this

is a bad time for you to be out. You know we've got the autograph party this afternoon, and I have an appointment with a sales rep this morning."

"You can't time a sore throat, Tiffany," Lois said reproachfully.

"I don't know," Tiffany muttered. "Didn't you stay home with one just last week?"

"I think this is a continuation. I probably never got over the other one."

Lois's voice sounded perfectly normal—no trace of laryngitis or evidence of difficulty in swallowing. Almost positive the woman's illness was faked, Tiffany decided to push a little. "Couldn't you come in for just an hour or so?"

"Do you want me to spread germs to your customers?"

"I'll take the chance. I need help badly."

"You know I'd come in if I could . . ."

No, I don't know that, Tiffany thought.

"But I really feel very bad."

Wearily, Tiffany said, "All right, Lois. Take care." She hung up the phone thoughtfully. Not only had Lois looked well last night, she had looked exceptionally *good*. She had color in her cheeks for once and some animation in her face. Could a bad sore throat come on *that* fast?

Tiffany shrugged. She'd muddle through somehow. She always had. But unsure now that she would have time during the day to change for the autograph party, after breakfast she dressed in a sheer black wool jumper and a white blouse with flowing poet sleeves. She could always dash upstairs or into the store washroom to renew her makeup, so she spent only a minimum of time on that. A dab of a light but spicy floral scent, and she was ready for what was shaping up as a long, hard day at the store.

Before starting the daily routine, Tiffany checked the store window. It contained hardcover copies of the Carrolls' three mystery novels, arranged in colorful pyramids the day before. Tiffany had included in the display an announcement of the autograph party and a picture of the Carrolls, a youngish-looking couple with humorous eyes, smiling fondly at each other.

How fortunate the Carrolls were! Tiffany thought wistfully. What a wonderfully close relationship they must have—discussing plots, giving helpful criticism, supporting each other.

She sighed, then briskly straightened the books in the window. At least she'd get to meet and talk with the charming couple.

The morning passed quickly in answering telephone inquiries and waiting on customers. The sales representative arrived during the pre-lunch lull, so Tiffany was able to go through the publisher's catalog with him and do her book ordering without interruption.

Lunch, immediately afterward, was an apple and a container of yogurt hastily snatched from the refrigerator upstairs. Tiffany freshened her makeup in the washroom and started to relax.

It was a feather in her cap to have the Carrolls come to her bookstore. Although they were popular mystery authors, they made very few public appearances. Book sales always jumped after an autograph party, and The Red Herring definitely could use more business. Another year as lean as the first might be the bookstore's last.

Tiffany checked the table that had been set up for the Carrolls. It held copies of their books and pens ready for the autographing. Behind this table was another containing an urn of coffee, a platter of tea sandwiches that Tiffany had made and frozen days before, cheese cubes, a plate of cookies that were sprinkled with red sugar to spell out *Devil's Due*, the title of the Carroll's latest best seller, and a gallon jug of white wine.

Shortly before the Carrolls were due to arrive, Tiffany was surprised to see Kirk Davis standing at a bookcase in the farthest corner of the store. He had an opened book in his hand and a sly smile on his face. It was obvious that he was waiting for her to discover him. He looked fresh and handsome in the same tweed jacket that he had worn that morning but with a different shirt, a fine cotton with narrow pink stripes, and a silk tie with a famous-name designer's crest on it. He also looked rested, as if he might have gotten a few hours sleep. Tiffany smiled to herself. It was nice, having a man dress up for you.

"Can I help you?" she asked.

Kirk grinned. "What did you have in mind?"

"I was thinking of a book."

"So was I, and all the titles have *love* in them," he crooned. Tiffany raised her eyebrows and bent forward to see what Kirk was reading. "Mm, you smell intriguing," he said. "Wear that tonight, and I won't answer for the consequences."

"Thanks for the warning—I won't. You're reading Dorothy Sayers!" Her voice was full of pleased surprise.

"I've been trying to figure out what this Peter Wimsey has that I don't," he told her.

"Class," Tiffany answered sweetly. When his eyes turned a sea-cold gray and flickered dangerously, her own brown ones narrowed with amusement. "He was an English lord," she explained.

Kirk accepted her explanation with a smile. "Where are your mystery authors? It's two o'clock."

Tiffany shrugged. "A few minutes late. Did you come to meet them or to watch the store?"

"Both." His voice softened. "And to see you."

He was moving too fast. To hold him off, Tiffany said coolly, "In addition to books, we have a fine selection of mystery games and puzzles you might like to examine while you're here. If you like, I'll show you where they are." She started to move away.

"Stay a while," he pleaded. "There isn't a customer in the place." He took her hand and put it on his smooth cheek. "I'll think you don't like me clean-shaven and all gussied up."

Tiffany put her head back and laughed—a spontaneous musical trill.

"You're lovely when you do that," Kirk murmured. He cupped her shoulders with his hands and put his lips to hers, stroking them lightly, nibbling gently at the corners, tasting them. Ripples of delight, each one greater than the last, spread through her.

She stirred in his gentle grasp, and his kiss deepened. His mouth twisted hungrily against hers, while his hands moved sensuously up and down the flowing silk sleeves, setting up a tingling friction against her skin.

He lifted his lips slightly and whispered, "Just wait till tonight."

Oh no, friend, Tiffany thought, you're not moving in on *this* poor defenseless widow. I know what you want. You're not the first man who's tried to play husband-for-a-night, although I have to admit you're the most attractive.

Even if your intentions *were* honorable, her thoughts continued ruefully, they'd have to stay just that—intentions. My New Year's resolutions are made for the rest of my life—never get involved again with a man in a dangerous occupation.

Tiffany started to pull away at the same time that Kirk drew her closer to him. They knocked against the bookcase, and all the mystery authors whose names began with *S* fell off the shelf in a barrage of sharp explosions.

"I think Lord Peter Wimsey just came a cropper."

"I'd appreciate your picking the books up," Tiffany answered in a fierce whisper. "Some customers just came in."

Kirk looked over his shoulder. "Carriage trade."

Two smartly dressed women hovered uncertainly inside the door. Tiffany greeted them with a comment about the pleasant weather and offered them refreshments while they waited for the Carrolls, who were expected momentarily. The ladies accepted the white wine with enthusiasm.

More people entered—but not the Carrolls. Tiffany had to put out more wine. And soon there was a steady stream of genteel sippers and browsers with cheese-smeared fingers, riffling through the books stacked for autographing.

"They're getting sloshed!" Tiffany said, horrified, to Kirk.

"It's a good party," he admitted with a grin. "This looks like your mystery couple now," he added under his breath. "And oh, wow!"

"Oh...wow," Tiffany echoed weakly. What had happened to her humorous, smiling youngish couple?

Nancy was a sweating, pallid woman, crowding sixty, with a bulky, shawl-draped body that she steered through the store like a battleship. When she finally docked at the autograph table, she took off a frayed straw *campesino* hat and, holding it by the broad brim, fanned herself. After a brief glance of distaste at the crowd, she pasted a sugary smile on her pale lips and bellowed, "We walked! Don't you have any cabs in this hick town? I'm parched. Nick, get me some water, or I won't be able to say a word."

"Get it yourself," roared Nick, a short, chunky, gravel-throated man waddling through the crowd in her wake.

"We have all kinds of refreshments," Tiffany interposed hurriedly. "Chilled white wine, hot coffee, soft drinks."

"Water will do, honey. I never imbibe."

Nick grunted at this.

"Mr. Carroll? What can I bring you?" Tiffany asked.

"He'll have water, too," Nancy announced in stentorian tones.

"Oh, Lord," Tiffany breathed as she passed Kirk on her way to get a carafe of water.

"When does the main bout begin?"

"Soon, I'm afraid. Hold the fort. I'll be right back."

Tiffany felt a surge of gratitude toward Kirk when she returned with the water. He had evidently mollified the Carrolls by addressing a question to them. People throughout the store had gathered at the autograph table

to hear the answer, and judging by the smiles on both
Nick and Nancy's faces, the question had been an agree-
able one. Moreover, first Nancy, who overflowed the
folding chair she was sitting on, and then Nick, who
looked rooted to his, accepted—more or less gra-
ciously—what seemed also to have been a compliment
from Kirk.

Or maybe they had just been holding out for water,
Tiffany thought with an inward groan. Because after
Nancy had slurped it, rolled it around in her mouth, and
done everything but gargle with it, and Nick had closed
his eyes and drunk it like medicine, everything was
downhill.

"How do you apportion the writing between you?"
one of the two designer-dressed matrons simpered. "Does
one of you do the murders and the other the detecting?"

"I write the books, and he types them," Nancy
trumpeted.

"Oh!" The woman exhaled as though all the air had
been knocked out of her. She backed away from the
autograph table, pulling her friend along by the arm. No
books and no money exchanged hands.

"Does it bother you to write about murder and killing
and violence all the time?" an earnest-faced student asked.

"Better to write about it than do it," Nick growled,
with a meaningful glance at Nancy.

"Your detective, Farragut, is an amateur, an inarti-
culate typing teacher from Fresno who chews raisins
constantly. I have two questions about that, sir," a girl
with a steno notebook said.

"*Shoot!*"

The girl recoiled, gripped her notebook, and plunged
on. "First, is it plausible that in *Death Notes*, Farragut
would leap from a burning building, land on his feet,
and reach for a raisin?"

"Well—" Nick started to reply.

"What do you want him to do, sugar? Reach for a
grapefruit?" Nancy interrupted.

"Nancy, I've warned you before about taking over press conferences," Nick scolded.

"This isn't a press conference," Nancy rapped out.

"Whatever it is, I don't like you taking over. Keep your trap shut or I'll tap you one on the jaw."

Nancy heaved her huge bulk off the chair. "I don't have to take that from you or anyone else," she bawled. "You can answer these dumb questions and autograph the books yourself. Thank God, you can sign your name." She sailed out, and Nick followed, waving his arms and screaming at her.

"Protector of poor little booksellers, keep me sane," Tiffany muttered. She hurried forward and apologized to the astonished crowd, blaming fatigue for the Carrolls' most unusual behavior.

Reaction was mixed. One woman announced that she'd rather read a cornflakes box than another Nick and Nancy Carroll. Others thought the incident was funny, but nobody was coming forward to buy a book.

"How good are those Carroll books?" Kirk whispered hurriedly to Tiffany.

"Surprisingly good, considering who writes them."

"Give me some adjectives."

"Logical, well-crafted, suspenseful, and—I believe—authentic."

Kirk stepped up to the autograph table. He moved his hands over the array of Carroll mystery novels and smiled disarmingly. "For what it's worth, I'm a police officer, and these Carroll books are good! They're exciting, full of suspense, authentic, and I only wish we had that typing teacher from Fresno solving cases for the SFPD. I wouldn't care what it cost the city in raisins."

Kirk paused while the audience laughed. "As you saw, due to the volatility of genius, the Carrolls left before they could autograph all the books you folks wanted to buy"—*any* of the books, Tiffany annotated silently—"but if you want my humble autograph, a member of San Francisco's Finest, so to speak, you've got it."

The crowd was amused—and charmed. Kirk's virile good looks and easy manner had erased the bad impression left by the Carrolls. A number of people bought books and had Kirk sign them. He stayed at the table all afternoon, autographing and patiently answering questions about police work, until the autograph party came to an official close at six o'clock.

"How can I thank you?" Tiffany said quietly as she looked at the respectably small number of Carroll books left.

Kirk grinned smugly. "You really want to know?"

Tiffany laughed. "I don't think so." She made a little face. "I'm not sure what you did was strictly honest. You hadn't read the books, but you made it seem that you had."

Kirk shrugged. "No one was harmed, and my autograph may be worth something some day."

"On a parking ticket?"

"How about a marriage license?"

"How about dinner? I'm starved. Those locusts swept all the food off the table before I could grab even a cheese cube."

"It's still early. Can you hold out while we have a drink first? I'll order something nourishing for you."

They went to a cocktail lounge at the top of a hotel with a view of the city. Kirk suggested a drink that was a colorful concoction of fruit and coconut juice and rum. Tiffany ate the orange slice right down to the rind, and the chunk of pineapple, and the bright red maraschino cherry.

"Hold it! Don't start chomping on the toothpick." Kirk got up and walked to a shining copper serving cart. When he returned, he was holding two small plates piled high with seafood appetizers. "Here, this should hold you over," he said with a smile. "I got us some giant prawns, a couple of crab legs, and oysters."

"Wonderful! Between the drink and these, I won't need to eat for a week."

"Save room for the best food in town."

"Not Dominick's!"

"The same."

"It's the place I dream about. How did you know?"

"I'm psychic."

"That must make you very useful on the police force."

"Right. I get all the poltergeist cases."

Tiffany sank back in her brown leather swivel chair and looked out the window. San Francisco—the bay, Golden Gate Bridge, and the city—lay spread out beneath them, its streets lit up and ready for a festive evening.

"It's a beautiful city," Tiffany said.

"It's my city."

"Mine, too. Owen and I lived in southern California, but this is where I belong."

"Well, at least we won't quarrel about where we're going to live." His voice held its usual half-humorous note, and his eyes twinkled blue as San Francisco's bay when the sun shone. Tiffany gave him a sidelong ironic look. Putting his finger on her chair, he swiveled her toward him and, leaning forward, folded his hands around hers. Tiffany looked down at them. Their smallness and whiteness made them look like flowers half-hidden in large, sun-browned leaves.

He doesn't even have to do anything, Tiffany thought. It's like a laying on of hands, all the warmth and strength and power in his flowing into mine. And back into his, she continued dreamily, back and forth between the two of us like an electric current. Her eyes closed. Let's put out the lights and go to . . .

"Tiffany!" His voice sounded overly loud.

Alarmed, she blinked her eyes open. "What's the matter?"

Kirk was smiling. "Nothing. Only, you're the first date who's fallen asleep on me."

"It's been a long day," Tiffany apologized.

"Go back to sleep, if you want. I don't plan to do

anything exciting—just now." He raised one of her hands
to his lips, and she was surprised that her hands had lain
in his all this while.

"You're pretty sure of yourself, aren't you, Detective
Davis?"

"I've had lots of experience in . . . let's say . . . community
relations."

His brash grin was irresistible. Tiffany smiled and
lowered her eyes until her long, dark lashes swept her
cheeks again.

Still holding her hand, Kirk put his lips to the smooth
flesh between her index and middle fingers. He darted
his tongue into the valley, then ran it lightly up the side
of her finger. Tiffany gasped at the unexpected stab of
excitement that went through her. He raised his eyes and
looked at her. "Let's go eat," he said quietly.

Dominick's was famous in a city known for its restaurants, and as the maître d' led them through a series
of rooms until they reached their table, Tiffany had to
admit that she was impressed. The tables set wide apart
and draped in the crispest and whitest napery, the large
crystal chandeliers in each room, the soft, thick carpeting, and the oil paintings on the walls all contributed to
an atmosphere of restrained opulence.

The waiter pulled the table out for her and Tiffany
seated herself on the plush banquette. Her limpid brown
eyes shone with curiosity. How could Kirk afford this
on a policeman's salary?

Kirk acknowledged her unasked question with a smug
smile. "If you're wondering if we'll be doing dishes for
our dinner, the answer is no." As she continued to look
at him questioningly, he said with a straight face, "I'm
on the take."

Tiffany knew he was joking, but even if she hadn't
surmised that, the last thing she would have associated
with Kirk Davis was crookedness. There seemed to be
too much tough integrity in the man for that.

She raised a skeptical eyebrow, and Kirk waved his

hand in a casual gesture. "I was lucky with some stocks I own."

"What's a nice guy like you doing on the police force, anyway?" Tiffany asked, with a teasing, mocking smile.

"That's why," Kirk answered evenly. "Because I *am* a nice guy. I don't like to see people pushed around, not anybody—not John Doe by a guy with a knife or gun, or the person on the other side of the law by brutal cops or guards. I have a bachelor's degree in social anthropology, and I plan to go on for an M.A. in criminology. Theory helps you keep your perspective, gain a broad view of things; but I'm an activist—I like to make things happen. That's why I'm a cop and a happy one."

They ordered then—Tiffany, from a menu without prices. She started with a plate of fresh asparagus served with a sauce maltaise, an orange-flavored hollandaise, and, because she had never had it, went on to *marcassin,* wild young boar. Kirk ordered the wines from the sommelier with confident decisiveness— a chilled Vouvray with the asparagus and a hearty red Burgundy for the meat. For dessert, they shared a warm, fluffy raspberry soufflé.

When they had finished eating and were waiting for Kirk's car to be brought around to the front door of the restaurant, Kirk put his arm around Tiffany's slim waist. "Feel better now?"

"Umm. That was the most heavenly meal I've ever had. I'm so full, I'll never make it up a hill."

"Just leave it to the master driver to get you home," Kirk boasted.

He drove like a native San Franciscan, taking his foot off the accelerator at precisely the right moment before topping the rise of each steep grade, so that he didn't shoot wildly over the top or stall and roll back. He exuded a sense of skill and power that Tiffany respected. And when he reached out his arm and pulled her close to him, a filament of hot, glowing excitement burned inside her as she wondered what would happen next.

Stopping the car in front of The Red Herring, Kirk

said, "That's a terrific effect you've created."

Tiffany smiled in the darkness beside him. The old Victorian house with its peaked roof, gables, and gingerbread trim was the very model of a haunted house. Tiffany had enhanced the impression by hanging windowshades painted with silhouetted figures: an old lady reading in a rocking chair, a man in a trenchcoat and fedora, and a black bat circling a tombstone.

"I like everything about it except the dim light in the store," Kirk continued. "Strong light's a deterrent to crime."

"But that would spoil the effect!"

"It might be worth it," Kirk said seriously as they got out of the car. Tiffany led the way to the side entrance and, once inside, up the staircase to her apartment, where she turned on a table lamp. "You really could use a couple of spots outside," Kirk insisted.

"Maybe I should get a police dog, a German shepherd, for the cat burglar."

"I'd say a police*man*."

They were standing so close, it would take only one long step for him to reach her. Waiting, Tiffany felt her heart stand still. She wanted his kiss—and she didn't want it. She was attracted to him—and she didn't want to be. In this single moment of time, she was living on as many levels as a big city department store.

First Floor: Men's Clothing, Notions, Perfumes. Second Floor: Sleepwear, Beauty Salon, Ladies Lounge.

As his lips descended to hers, what she saw made her step back and place a delaying finger on his mouth.

"Your eyes!" Tiffany exclaimed.

"Still two, I hope." He removed her finger and brought his lips close again.

"No, it's not that." She placed her hand on his mouth once more and gazed with rapt interest into his eyes. "It's simply amazing how they change color. They're gray for when you're a cop, blue when you're amused, and . . ."

"What color are they now?"

"Green," Tiffany answered with awe in her voice. "Greener than I've ever seen them before."

"Suppose we do something about it before they change color again," Kirk said, his voice smoky and low. Firmly, he removed her hand from his mouth. Then he pulled her toward him with an authority she had no desire to dispute. She closed her eyes, shutting out all awareness of everything except his mouth covering hers in hungry, rapacious kisses that went on and on without stopping till neither of them could breathe and they broke apart.

"Tiffany!" he murmured. "You wonderful, wonderful woman."

He pressed her eyelids delicately with his lips, making of each a dew-touched poppy. Then he buried his face in the sweep of hair that covered her right cheek and playfully tugged at her earlobe with his teeth. He trailed his lips down the white velvet of her throat and stole under her blouse until he found the little hollow just above her collarbone.

Inviting his hot, marauding mouth, Tiffany arched her slender neck and groaned inwardly at the exquisite pleasure each kiss gave her. His hands slid between her arms and her sides, grazing her breasts. With one hand splayed across her back, he let the other follow the curve of her breast while he pulled her closer. Responding to the need he had aroused in her, Tiffany thrust her hips forward against his. Then bells went off in her mind.

Third Floor: Bridal Salon. Fourth Floor: Infants and Children's Wear. Going Up.

Tiffany pulled away from him. "Kirk, I can't handle this. Please."

"Tiffany—"

"No, I think you'd better go. It's been a wonderful evening, but it's late and I have a big day planned for tomorrow."

He stepped back and let his arms drop. "Sorry, I thought . . ."

"I know what you thought." Tired and exacerbated by the events of her working day and upset at having to reject this man she so wanted, Tiffany again defensively lumped Kirk in with all those dates who had a single reflexive response when they'd learned she was a widow. To her own surprise, she heard herself murmuring, "A poor defenseless widow." She meant it mostly as a joke, but it sounded instead like an accusation.

"You should see me with orphans," Kirk said bitterly. He strode to the door. "Good night, Tiffany. Lock the door."

Then he was gone. Tiffany wandered around the room, touching things aimlessly, amazed at how fast the whole thing happened. It had taken no more than a spark for them to be in each other's arms; no more than a spark for a quarrel.

She wanted him back. She wanted to run her fingers over his smooth cheek and feel the sharp bones underneath. She wanted the excitement of watching his eyes change color and knowing she was in danger.

Her fingers went to her lips. His kisses were changeable, too. Sometimes she could barely feel their soft, clinging pressure. Other times they burned with his fury to possess her.

Tiffany picked a velvet sofa pillow up off the floor and crushed it between her hands, as if the outlet for her unhappiness was coming not in tears but in the release of kinetic energy. Then, decisively, she dropped the pillow to the floor.

Kirk was attractive and interesting, and she liked him. He made her blood sing and her spirits soar. He was exciting. He put pizzazz in her day.

But there was nowhere for their relationship to go. Casual encounters weren't for her. She didn't love him, and thank heavens she didn't, because never, never again would she let herself in for the anguish of loving a man whose morning "so long" could mean "good-bye forever." And with that electricity of attraction between them like a spark jumping from terminal to terminal, friendship was impossible.

She had to say one thing for Bennett Powell, Tiffany

reflected: He might not carry much voltage, but he was safe. The only thing teachers at Gifford Sage died of was old age.

With a deep sigh, she prepared for bed. She would see Bennett tomorrow. He had promised to accompany her on the mystery walk she was leading. What a laugh Detective Sergeant Kirk Davis would get out of *that*— a bunch of armchair detectives retracing the steps of Sam Spade.

Chapter 4

"IT'S GOOD OF you to come, Bennett," Tiffany said. They were standing alone in Union Square at the foot of the granite Spanish-American War column.

"Not at all. A *Maltese Falcon* walk gives me the chance to see you. There aren't always that many opportunities." Bennett's look was humorously reproachful.

Tiffany smiled sympathetically and touched Bennett's arm. "The store keeps me busy."

But even her apology took on a vague, abstracted air as she looked around her at the people who populated the scene: businessmen taking short cuts through the park, well-dressed women hurrying to the fashionable department stores that ringed the square, and tourists leaving the venerable St. Francis Hotel across the way for a day of sightseeing.

Arms over their faces, a few bums curled up on the benches, oblivious to passersby and the pigeons that whirred over their heads before landing in new alignments on the cement walks.

"Looking for someone?" Bennett asked politely.

"Just the first arrivals." *And maybe a glimpse of him!*
Tiffany frowned. That was a bad sign, searching crowds
for a certain face. She glanced at her watch. "Five to ten
and no one's here yet. But, then, we didn't start last
year's walk until about ten minutes after the hour."

"You should start on time," Bennett reproved her.

"I know," Tiffany sighed, "but I don't have the heart
to disappoint people."

Then everyone seemed to come at once, and by ten
past ten, Tiffany had a group of twenty-five people gathered around her. Some were members of the Followers
or customers of The Red Herring. Others were strangers,
people interested in Dashiell Hammett, the author of *The
Maltese Falcon,* or in mysteries in general. Walking
groups like this occasionally picked up one of the city's
oddballs, too, and Tiffany was glad Bennett was along
to steer off such people.

Tiffany started the tour by giving a brief biography
of Hammett, followed by a synopsis of *The Maltese
Falcon* for those in the crowd who might not have read
the book or seen the famous movie with Humphrey Bogart. She pointed to the St. Francis and announced that
it was believed to have been the red-carpeted lobby of
that hotel from which detective Miles Archer started the
shadowing job that resulted in his death and involvement
of his partner, Sam Spade, in the chase after the bejew-
eled black falcon.

Tiffany then led her group up Powell Street to Burritt
Alley off Bush Street. This was the most famous Hammett landmark in San Francisco. The bronze plaque on
the side of the wall told the story: "On approximately
this spot, Miles Archer, partner of Sam Spade, was done
in by Brigid O'Shaughnessy."

Tiffany stopped for a long time here to discuss the
significance of this event, the first murder in *The Maltese
Falcon* and the one that caused Sam Spade's commitment, because by Spade's code a man had to do something when his partner was killed. Passersby stopped to

stare and sometimes to listen, but Tiffany ignored them.

It was only when she noticed a man in a woolen watch cap over long, straight brown hair, a ripped leather flight jacket, and grubby jeans, that she became flustered. Which just goes to show what you can do with rags! she thought, rolling her eyes upward. She realized now that Kirk had probably followed the group from Union Square and that she had been too busy answering the questions of a mystery buff from Burbank to see him standing at the edge of the crowd.

"There's that bum again, the one who was hanging around the bookstore the night I gave my talk," Bennett said. "I'll get rid of him." A warning look on Kirk's face as Bennett approached him stopped Tiffany from telling Bennett who Kirk really was. "Move along, man, you're bothering these people here," big Bennett Powell commanded.

"It's a free country," Kirk answered truculently. "Am I bothering you, lady?" he appealed to Tiffany. She glared at him, but it did no good. His eyes were as blue as California skies now, and a barely hidden mischievous smile lit their depths.

"He's all right," Tiffany said to Bennett. "You can stay if you like," Tiffany told Kirk coolly.

"Thanks, lady. For a minute there, I thought you were going to pull a Brigid O'Shaughnessy on me."

The crowd laughed.

"Miles Archer was a *detective*, not a—"

"Bum," Kirk interrupted. "Go ahead and say it, lady, it doesn't bother me. Sounds like you have a thing for detectives," Kirk continued with a sly look.

"It's fun *reading* about their exploits," Tiffany admitted haughtily.

"How about their exploits in the flesh?" Kirk's lips twitched with suppressed laughter.

"It's time to move along now," Tiffany said sternly to her tour group, who were obviously fascinated by this lady-and-the-tramp exchange. "I'm going to show you the hotels where much of the action of *The Maltese Falcon* takes place. Although the names are different from those Hammett used for them, the hotels themselves are fairly easy to identify. After that, we'll see other places mentioned in the novel or identified as the locales of the scenes."

As the tour continued up and down the hills of San Francisco, Kirk walked beside Tiffany. People in the group turned their heads away and smiled, and Bennett scowled, but Kirk paid no attention.

"Do you mind telling me just why you're doing this?" Tiffany asked testily.

"Information. There's a whole other world out there I know nothing about—the world of the hard-boiled detective with a heart of gold."

"Sam Spade didn't have a heart of gold. He turned in the woman he loved."

"I'd never do that to you."

"You wouldn't have the chance. I don't go around shooting people with Webley Fosbery automatic revolvers."

"So that's what Brigid used? That reminds me, you'll have to come up and see my gun collection sometime."

Tiffany gave him a withering look. "Don't you have work to do? In fact, aren't you on duty now? Those look like your work clothes."

"*My* version of the pinstripe and button-down oxford," Kirk murmured.

But Tiffany wasn't listening. How stupid she had been! Kirk was on duty! Obviously, he had his eye on someone in The Red Herring crowd, but who? The people she knew on the tour were mostly librarians and teachers and accountants. There was a lawyer among them and a pair of widows. And of course Bennett Powell.

The thought that solid Bennett might be suspected of being a cat burglar struck Tiffany as so funny that she exploded in a little laugh, and Bennett himself glanced up from the sidewalk he had been perusing to give her a sour look. Contrite, she smiled at him, and he fell in step beside her, with Kirk remaining on her other side.

"What are you doing walking with that bum? Why don't you let me get rid of him?" he whispered.

Some imp made Tiffany say, "I'm rehabilitating him."

"Don't be funny, Tiffany. This guy could be the cat burglar who's been terrorizing the neighorbood. He's probably been weaseling information out of you."

"He'd have a hard time being a cat *and* a weasel."

"What's gotten into you?" Bennett was really annoyed now and not bothering to disguise the fact.

Bennett was no fool. She *did* feel lighthearted and gay, and his noticing it made Tiffany realize with sudden poignancy that she wasn't often like this. She looked at the man on her right. Her eyes fell on the hole in the knee of his jeans, the sandal strap tied with a grubby shoelace, the bare feet that had picked up the grime of San Francisco's sidewalks. And she felt happy, as Bennett in his tweed jackets and V-neck pullovers never made her feel.

"It must be the beautiful day—the clear, brisk air and sunshine."

"It's just typical San Fran weather," Bennett grumbled.

"But I love it. It's intoxicating and habit-forming. I couldn't live anywhere else."

"Neither could I," Kirk chimed in.

"Sure," Bennett said sharply. "Anywhere else, it'd be too cold to loll around on the streets and sleep in parks. That's why we've got so many derelicts here." Bennett strode off angrily to the rear of the group.

Kirk grinned. "Sometimes I think he doesn't like me. Listen, how about going on a double date with me tonight—dinner at the best place in North Beach, the Caffè Venezia. The other couple are friends of mine—Tom and Gina Laughlin. He's a fellow cop, and his wife's a nurse. They're great people. You'd like them."

"I don't think I'll be able to go. Thanks anyway, Kirk."

"Sam Spade ate at the Venezia."

"I happen to know that Sam Spade did not eat in North Beach."

"And boy, did he regret it! The Venezia has the best linguine with red clam sauce in town. Do you like linguine with red clam sauce?"

Tiffany hesitated. *Why can't I tell a lie and say no, I don't like it? What am I, the George Washington of linguine with red clam sauce?*

"If it's really good," she temporized.

"This is the best. Pick you up at six-thirty? We'll have a drink at Gina and Tom's place first. They've been dying to meet you."

"Why?" Tiffany asked flatly.

"I dunno. I suppose it's because of what I've been telling them about you. I'll tell *you* some day—if you're nice to me." Then, with a grin like the Cheshire Cat's, he disappeared into the crowd.

The tour ended with lunch at a restaurant that featured Hammett memorabilia—a continuous three-wall row of still photos with dialogue captions from the movie *The Maltese Falcon,* pictures of people associated with Hammett, books about the author, and even a statuette of the famous black bird itself.

When the group started to sit down at long tables in a private room, Bennett put himself next to Tiffany. "Is there anything funny going on between you and that bum?" he asked plaintively.

It distressed Tiffany to be less than candid with Bennett, but for Kirk's sake she had to be. So she answered coolly, "Don't be ridiculous. It's interesting to get another point of view once in a while, that's all."

"Point of view! How about hardened criminals? Dope addicts?"

"They're coming next," Tiffany teased.

Bennett turned away and stabbed a breaded scallop on his plate. "What do you say we go out tonight—have dinner, take in a show?"

"I'd love to—another time. But I've already made plans for the evening."

"Exploring the lower depths of San Francisco?" Bennett said sarcastically.

"Right. The opium dens of Chinatown."

Bennett stabbed another scallop, then pushed it viciously around his plate.

"They're dead, you know," Tiffany said mildly. "You don't have to kill them."

Bennett looked at her. "What?"

"The scallops. You were committing mayhem on them."

He let his fork drop with a clatter. Tiffany was surprised. It wasn't like Bennett to make a scene. "I don't know what's the matter with you, Tiff. The last few days you haven't been a bit like yourself."

"Isn't that good—sometimes to be not oneself?"

Bennett picked up his fork again. "Let's not be simplistic," he said scornfully, lifting a scallop and balancing it judiciously at the end of his fork. "You know I'm against conventionality for its own sake, but a certain consistency of behavior is expected of adults."

"Is it?" Tiffany asked dreamily. She was thinking of the way Kirk had looked as he walked off. He didn't make a very good derelict. There was too much leashed energy in that well-knit, muscular body; too much elasticity in his stride.

Becoming aware then of Bennett's disapproving stare, Tiffany brought the other people at the table and Bennett himself into focus again. It occurred to her that they didn't know Kirk wasn't actually a bum. Tiffany smiled to herself. Didn't that, in a way, make Kirk her secret lover?

By the time Tiffany got back to The Red Herring, it was midafternoon. A man held the door open for her. She smiled and thanked him, then started searching her memory for where she had seen him before. His salon-dressed hair and smooth features, coupled with a three-piece business suit, could have belonged to any one of a number of San Franciscans.

Then Tiffany remembered. He was the man she thought

of as "Pinky Ring," because that was his only distin-
guishing feature. He was the junior exec type who had
come to Bennett's Sherlock Holmes talk.

Lois was ringing up a cash sale. "How was the great
Sam Spade walk?" she asked Tiffany with a smile. "Ms.
Bradford conducts a walk through San Francisco showing
some of the locales in *The Maltese Falcon*," Lois explained to the customer standing before her.

Tiffany said that the walk had been good.

"How were things here?" she asked when the customer
left.

Lois shook her head. "Slow."

Tiffany reflected again on how vibrant and happy the
older woman looked.

"I hate to tell you this," Lois went on, "but you've
got mice again—maybe even rats."

A chill ran through Tiffany. She could feel herself
turning pale. It might be irrational, but there it was. She
had a phobia about mice. She had the proverbial Victorian vapors when she saw a rodent. When she gave
gifts to the children of friends, she rejected furry wind-
up mice, and never bought them books about darling
little mouse families. She even flatly refused invitations
to *The Nutcracker* ballet at holiday time, and refused to
read "The Pied Piper of Hamlin."

"The basement?" Tiffany asked, shuddering.

Lois nodded, her small dark eyes rather like a rodent's
themselves, Tiffany thought.

"Well, call the exterminator," she told her assistant
wearily.

"That isn't necessary. I'll put some poison around."

"Don't you mind?" Tiffany looked at her with wonder.

"No, I did it the last time. Remember?"

"And it didn't work. They're back. I think perhaps
this time we'd better have an exterminator."

"No need to go to that expense," Lois insisted. "You
can't help them coming back in an old house like this.
Don't worry, I'll keep after 'em this time." She added
with a broad smile, "Just stay out of the basement."

Tiffany shuddered again. "Don't worry, I will." She grimaced for emphasis. "By the way, it's all right with me if you take off now. You might want to pick up what you'll need for the basement so that you can start using it as soon as you come in tomorrow."

"Thanks. I really appreciate that, Tiffany." Lois reached beneath the counter and pulled out a brown leather portfolio.

Tiffany stared at it. "Doesn't that belong to the man who just left? I can't remember whether he had it with him today, but he had one just like it at Bennett's talk the other night."

Lois laughed. "There must be a million of these in the city. I brought it to the store because I'm working on my own mystery novel, and I planned a trip to the library this evening to do a little research."

"How interesting! I didn't know you were writing."

"Writing but not getting published," Lois said wryly. "See you tomorrow, Tiffany."

How little one knew about people, Tiffany mused. Lois had been working for her almost a year, and Tiffany hadn't known that she was writing a book.

At six o'clock, Tiffany put the CLOSED sign on the front door and ran upstairs to her own apartment. She looked apprehensively at the old wooden floors and closets, then decided not to think about mice. She could readily forgive Lois her absences in consideration of her unusual, unlooked-for willingness to act as The Red Herring's official rodent catcher.

Tiffany dressed quickly, exchanging one suit for another—a bright red wool for the businesslike tan gabardine she had worn for the walking tour—and an ivory silk blouse for a white cotton shirt with a black bow. She brushed her hair out into a fluff of golden brown and applied fresh makeup, choosing evening shades that made her eyes dark and mysterious.

When the bell rang at the side entrance to the house, she grabbed her purse and ran down the stairs. "I'm ready," she called out breathlessly, wondering herself how she had done it.

"So am I!" Kirk said as she opened the door. His tone was humorous, but the ardent glow in his eyes made Tiffany's heart skip an extra beat. He always made her feel excited, as though she were in a situation that was dangerous but not threatening; one that would thrill but not harm her. Then his expression changed and he said sternly, "Still opening your door to strangers?"

"I knew it was you," she half-explained, half-apologized.

"Oh, yeah? And suppose Jack the Ripper had preceded me by about five minutes?"

"You would have caught him and gotten a promotion!" Tiffany answered triumphantly. "You could have afforded a new torn jacket, more ragged jeans, maybe sandals made out of rubber tires instead of cheap leather."

Kirk took her arm as they walked out to the car. "Don't make fun of my threads. They get results."

"You haven't caught the cat burglar yet," Tiffany taunted.

"Just give me time. He hasn't made a move recently."

"He must fence the stuff somewhere. Have you followed that lead?"

"The department's working on it," Kirk said dryly. "If we don't turn up anything, we'll call in Nero Wolfe."

On the drive to Daly City, where the Laughlins had just bought a house, Kirk, with his usual directness, launched immediately into the subject on his mind. "How close are you and that guy who knows how many cups of tea Sherlock Holmes drank every day?"

"I assume you mean Professor Bennett Powell." Tiffany leaned heavily on the word *professor*.

"That's who," Kirk answered cheerfully.

"Bennett's been a good friend to me. It was his idea to start the Followers of the Red Herring. He comes to all the meetings and delivers frequent talks like the one you heard."

"He's in love with you," Kirk said quietly.

"I know."

He glanced at her briefly, sternly. "Well, do you love him?"

"We have a lot in common," she temporized. Could Bennett be her defense against the turmoil Kirk caused in her? Did she even love Bennett—a little? She liked him a lot. They had common interests. Did feelings like that turn into love eventually? Or did one always long for a devilish pirate type like Kirk Davis? "Shall we let it ride, Kirk?" she said finally.

"Sure," he answered out the side of his mouth. Tiffany smiled. Kirk wasn't so different from Sam Spade as he thought.

The Laughlins' house was one of a row of nearly identical medium-sized stucco homes on a curving dead-end street. There was a rectangle of brown dirt in front, fenced off with string from the children riding tricycles on the sidewalk. White rags had been tied to the string to keep birds away from the grass seed. No shrubbery or trees or flowers had been planted yet.

But if the exterior was stark, the inside of the spanking-new house had been made warm and inviting. Window curtains were up, green plants supplied what the yard still lacked, and the furniture was old and comfortable.

The Laughlins had bought the house because, as a shining-eyed Gina told Tiffany, "Tom and I are going to start a family soon. Any day now," she said, laughing, "the doctor's going to say, 'Gina, you're going to have a baby.' Right, Tommy?"

Red-haired, tall, bony Tom Laughlin said with a laugh, "I'm doing *my* bit."

"Come, Tiffany, I'll show you the baby's room while Tom fixes us a drink. Just give him your order." Tiffany asked for a glass of white wine and followed the slender, dark-haired Gina down a short hall to a bedroom in the back. "All we've got in it so far is a picture." Gina switched on the light. "It's a sunny room and quiet, so the baby will be able to sleep. Sometimes Tommy has night duty and has to sleep days, so it would be better if the baby didn't wakc him up."

A chill invaded Tiffany. What if something happened to Tom Laughlin and this room remained empty, with the picture of a woolly white lamb under a fleecy blue and white sky to remind the warm, vivacious woman next to her of what might have been?

As if guessing her thought, Gina put her hand on Tiffany's arm and said quietly, "Let's go back to the men before they find a football game on TV. Then it'll be the Flying Pizza and all the beer in the fridge instead of a good time out."

Tiffany laughed and returned to the living room with Gina. She caught Kirk's look as she entered. It was so tender and so affectionate that, overwhelmed, she raised her chin and looked away. In doing so, she saw that Tom had intercepted Kirk's expression. His own look was an alloy of careful study and cautious interest, and Tiffany wondered what it meant.

Gina had been very open and almost instantly intimate with her. Not only was Gina dreaming of a baby to bless her and Tom's four-year marriage, it was obvious that she was hearing wedding bells for Tiffany and Kirk. She had assumed that Tiffany was Kirk's "girl," and no laughing disclaimer from Tiffany seemed to have changed her opinion.

"They think I'm your girl," Tiffany whispered to Kirk when Tom disappeared into the kitchen for another highball for himself and Kirk, and Gina joined him for more crackers for the cheese and homemade salami she was serving.

"I know," Kirk answered smugly. "I told them you were."

"Well, untell them," she snapped. "It's not true and it's embarrassing."

"I sometimes confuse present and future," Kirk said teasingly.

"How about past? As in, 'it's been nice knowing you.'"

"How about actions speak louder than words?" Kirk took Tiffany's hand and kissed the inside of her wrist. Playful as the kiss was, it set up a tingling thrill within her. Not noticing that Tom and Gina had entered the room, she let her hand remain in Kirk's for the sheer pleasure of its warm pressure on her skin.

"Uh-oh, sorry, lovebirds," Gina said with a laugh. Tom said nothing, and his pale blue eyes were inscrutable. A short while later, however, when they all started talking about it possibly being time to leave for the restaurant, he said to Tiffany, "I have a couple of books in the den that might interest you. They're paperback first editions of mysteries. Would you like to see them?"

"Very much!" Tiffany rose and left with Tom as Gina laughingly said, "Maybe I should be jealous. He never wanted to show *me* his first editions."

The small den was furnished in Early American style. The rocker, desk, and sofa-sleeper were of hard maple. There was a hooked rug on the floor, and Tiffany guessed that the curtains, a café-style print, had been made by Gina.

"Here are the books." Tom took three slim, fragile paperbooks encased in plastic out of a maple bookcase. "They're not worth much. When I bought them, I thought I might start a collection of out-of-print detective fiction, but I discovered I wasn't that interested so I stopped with these three." When they were in her hands, he said, "You can keep them if you want. Sell them in your store—I don't care. They're yours," he added quickly as she started to remonstrate.

"That's very kind of you, Tom. Can we make an exchange? Would you like to come to The Red Herring and pick out a few contemporary mysteries?"

Tom laughed. "No, thanks. I'm like Kirk. I get enough of that all day without reading about it, too." He fixed her with an appraising stare. "But I guess it's pretty important to you."

"It's my livelihood," Tiffany said a little sharply, not

liking this interrogation by an almost complete stranger. "And yes, I like it. That's why I opened a mystery bookstore."

"Kirk tells me you're a widow."

"That's right," she said quietly, wondering what he was getting at.

"He likes you a lot."

"Really, Tom," Tiffany said with a laugh, "did you bring me in here to ask if my intentions toward Kirk are honorable?"

To her surprise, he opened up and said "Yes, in a way." Tiffany looked at him for a long minute. "Kirk and I are friends from way back," he explained. "Before he got on the force, he was security guard for a very wealthy San Francisco family. He fell in love with the daughter, and the family made mincemeat of him. They fired him, wouldn't give him a reference, and gave him a bad rep in town."

"How about the girl? Did she love him?"

"She was a spoiled brat out for kicks—in this case, a real honest-to-goodness man instead of the society punks she ran around with."

"What does that have to do with me?" Tiffany asked quietly.

"Kirk's wised up a lot since then," Tom answered slowly. "But he hasn't fallen for anybody, either. When you store up a lot of emotion inside you the way Kirk's done, it becomes very strong. All I'm saying is, don't make any promises you can't keep."

"I never make promises I can't keep." Dropping the books on the desk, Tiffany marched out of the den, and two spots of angry color burned on her cheeks.

It was time to leave for North Beach then, and Tom and Gina excused themselves to make a last-minute check of doors and windows.

"What did Tom say to make you so mad?" Kirk asked.

"He was defending your honor," Tiffany said shortly.

A slow grin spread across Kirk's lean, intense face.

"And here I've been trying to lose it to you. With friends like Tom, who needs enemies?"

Tiffany's laugh cleared the air. She liked Kirk's friends. Gina's warmth and gaiety were irresistible. And Tiffany admired Tom's loyalty, even if she couldn't yet feel close to him. Above all, she didn't want any animosity between them, and it was obvious that Tom didn't, either. The result was that they left the house in high spirits, ready for a good time.

"How are we riding tonight?" Kirk asked when they got to his car. "Low class, middle class, or high class?"

"Which is which?" Tom asked.

"Low class—the men ride in front, the women in back; middle class—one couple in front, one in back; and high class..." Kirk paused for dramatic effect.

Going along with the joke, Gina said, "Yes?"

"High class," Kirk repeated, "they trade partners."

Laughing, Tom and Gina chose middle class.

"Lucky for you," Kirk said, "because that's what you were going to get anyway. I'm not taking Tiffany out so she can gossip in the back seat with Gina or have Tom tell her all the wild things I've done."

"What wild things have you done?" Tiffany asked as Kirk slid his muscular body behind the wheel.

Grinning, Kirk said, "I take the Fifth."

"Then I guess I'll just have to wait to find out, won't I?"

"If you're interested." He shot her a look in the semi-darkness.

"I'm interested," she admitted in a small, reluctant voice.

"Then I suppose someday you'll find out," he answered lightly.

As they drove back to the city, Tiffany wondered what it was that Kirk didn't want her to know.

Chapter 5

DEPENDING ON YOUR point of view, Tiffany reflected, the Saturday night crowd in North Beach was raucous, vulgar, and low, or vital and colorful. The neon signs of sex shows and nightclubs on Broadway cast a lurid glow on the faces of strolling tourists, sailors, and punks sporting bright green or purple furrows of hair riding bare scalps in Mohican haircuts.

But "topless" wasn't the only lure on Broadway. City Lights Books, once the center for the literati of the Beat generation who flocked to North Beach in the 1950's, was still open for business and drawing in crowds.

In contrast, the side streets were a quiet mixture of *caffès,* corner groceries with Italian names, and bakeries advertising Italian pastries. Over the motley scene floated the illuminated twin towers of Saints Peter and Paul Church, frosting the black sky with wedding-cake Gothic.

The Caffè Venezia was a small unpretentious place with red and white checked tablecloths, a thick white candle guttering in a wax-encrusted wine bottle at each table, and scenes of Venice on the walls. It was crowded, noisy, and cozy, and Tiffany loved it.

"I don't even care what the food's like," she said with a laugh, in answer to Gina's anxious question. "It's my kind of place." She looked at the animated faces around her, at the people laughing and talking as they ate, gesticulating with their forks or hands to drive a point home. "It's so lively and real," she said. So different from the world of books, she felt like adding.

"The food's good, too," Gina said. "I've been coming here since I was a little girl."

"Did you grow up in North Beach?" Tiffany asked.

"Yes. It was practically all Italian then. Now the Chinese are spreading out from Chinatown into the area. Which makes it typically San Francisco—the racial and cultural mix, I mean."

"And that mix makes for darn good eating," Kirk said. "I've had everything from ground beef tongue fried with sweet bananas in a Nicaraguan restaurant to hot dogs and beans in an all-nitery. Speaking of food . . ."

A waiter bustled over, and they all agreed to have wine. The house wine was an Italian vintage none of them had ever heard of, so, excited at the prospect of making a discovery, they decided on that. The wine was brought, uncorked, tasted, and okayed by Kirk, then poured into each glass.

Gina raised her glass. "To a new, rest-of-our-lives friendship," she said, looking with fond, laughing eyes at Tiffany.

They all clinked glasses, then each turned serious over the blackboard menu that the waiter put on their table.

At Gina's recommendation, they chose for their entrée veal scallopine alla Marsala accompanied by the famous linguine with red clam sauce. The work of ordering done, and with her eyes dark and sparkling over her wineglass, Gina continued the conversational theme she had begun. "You're with a bunch of all North Beachers tonight, Tiffany. I was born and grew up here. Tom's father walked a beat here. And Kirk's dad . . ."

"*Was* a beat here," Kirk interrupted. Although he

smiled as he said it, his eyes, Tiffany noticed, were that cold gray that meant all was not well within. "That's true," he added, addressing Tiffany alone. "My father left a college teaching career in the Midwest and came out here because he wanted to be with kindred spirits, people who—like him—wanted to apprehend the poetry of being, as they put it, to know all emotions and sensations, to experience everything, take it into themselves—not intellectually but directly. They wanted to be *beat*, which was Jack Kerouac's shorthand for *beatific*. But I guess you know all about the Beat generation," Kirk finished with a wry smile.

"I know something about them," Tiffany said softly, "but I don't know about your dad. What happened to him?"

"Oh, he didn't do too badly at first. He had some poetry published, did a little teaching, and a lot of hanging out at coffee houses. He sent for me and my mother—another free spirit," he explained with a humorous-sad weariness. "Only, out here with their new way of life, they didn't know what to do with me. I mean, a kid sort of cramped their style." Kirk smiled and shook his head at the wonder of this. Tiffany had the impression that the hurt had pretty much healed. "Luckily for me, Tom's dad took me in tow—made a man out of me, right, Tom?"

Now it was Tom's turn to laugh and shake his head at a story that seemed to have become a legend among the three friends. "I'll never forget the day Dad brought you home. You were wearing some old mess of a jacket two sizes too big for you, with the silk sun of Japan sewn on the back. You didn't have any socks, and it was cold. Your feet were dirty and Dad told me to make sure you had a bath and give you some of my clothes to wear—*good* clothes, he stressed, for self-respect—while he made dinner. My mother had died," Tom explained to Tiffany, "and Dad was raising me alone. But I was a *good* boy," Tom said jokingly, looking at Kirk, "responsible, diligent, punctual."

"A regular Boy Scout," Kirk grumbled.

"Anyway, Kirk practically moved in with us." Tom's face became somber. "And after a while, he actually did."

"What Tom didn't tell you, Tiffany," Kirk said, "is that his dad rescued me from a life that would eventually have landed me in reform school. I had been stealing, playing truant, hanging out with a bad crowd, most of whom ended up on drugs or in jail."

"Dad figured as long as he was bringing up one boy, he might as well handle two," Tom put in. "Besides, I think I was getting to be something of a prig."

"Faithful, diligent, trustworthy, punctual . . ." Kirk recited with a grin. "Anyway, to cut a long story short, Tom Laughlin, Sr. showed me another side of the law and of society—orderliness, respect for one's self and one's body, respect for other people and their property. I stayed in school, went to college, and decided to apply what I had learned by becoming a cop—always a couple of steps behind Tom here, who was already on the force."

"What happened to the others in the story?" Tiffany asked gently.

"My dad has retired from the force and complains every time we visit him because we haven't made him a grandpa yet," Tom said with a smile in Gina's direction.

"And my folks went on to Haight-Ashbury and what in the end amounted to self-destruction. That's when I moved in with the Laughlins." Kirk smiled serenely at Tiffany, as if to say, "It all turned out all right. Don't take it too seriously."

The story clarified a lot of things about Kirk. It explained the aura of toughness that seemed to come from something deeper than his experiences as a street cop and detective. It also explained his compassion, his acceptance of the fact that people's lives often turned out different from the way they had intended.

But most of all, Tiffany realized that Kirk's childhood was a closed chapter, as was her widowhood. Her impulse to joy reasserted itself, and she felt a tender glow at having been taken into this little family and entrusted with Kirk's life story.

The entreé arrived then and, as Gina had promised, was excellent. They topped it off with almond ice cream and macaroons for dessert, and followed that with tiny white cups of very strong, very black, thick espresso.

What with the wine, good food, and lively conversation, along with the warmth and vitality of the restaurant, the two couples were in a genial mood when they had finished. Out on the sidewalk again, they decided to walk off the rich meal and struck out through the crowded streets.

Kirk put his arm around Tiffany's waist, tightening his grip when he had to steer her around an obstacle, loosening it when the way was clear. But Tiffany was always aware of the sinewy pressure of his hand against her body. She liked the way they moved together, keeping the same pace in long, coordinated steps.

"You're a good walker," Kirk said.

"Climber's more like it. I used to go up and down Nob Hill every day."

"So that's why you're called Tiffany. I wondered."

"We didn't *live* there. When I was in college, I tutored a girl who did. Cable-car fare cut into the pittance I earned, so I hoofed it."

"What happened to the girl?"

"I'd like to be able to say she went on to Berkeley and a Nobel, but actually she barely made it into any percentile on the SAT and ended up at Gifford Sage."

"That's where your friend Bennett Powell, the guy who counts how many times Sam Spade sneezed, teaches, isn't it?"

"Yes, and you're being mean. There's nothing wrong with making mysteries your hobby. It's harmless, keeps people off the streets, and—"

"Keeps them buying books," Kirk interrupted.

"Which I supply. Right. And that's honest and legal." Tiffany laughed a little. "But not profitable—not yet, anyway."

"So now we're back to why you were named Tiffany."

"Mom thought Tiffany sounded ritzy. I think what she had in mind was a madcap heiress. What she forgot was to provide the money that went with the name. It was only in his later years after I had left home that Dad made enough in his stationery store to pick up pieces of rental property here and there, fix them up, and sell them. With the pricey real-estate market in San Francisco, he could sell the house I'm in for a nice sum of money, but he won't slip the rug out from under me, so to speak. I can hardly wait for the store to start making money for me to pay him a fair rent."

"You could make the place more attractive, more inviting to customers."

Tiffany was shocked. She had hired an experienced store planner to adapt the entire ground floor of the house to bookstore purposes and had spent weeks going over blueprints with him. "I think it's *very* inviting," she said indignantly.

Kirk pressed her waist slightly. "*You* are; the store isn't. I'll show you what I mean when I take you home."

Tiffany pondered what Kirk had said. She didn't like his interference, and she doubted that he could do any better than the expert she had hired. But she was also curious about his ideas for her store.

Tom insisted that he and Gina could go home on BART, the Bay Area Rapid Transit subway, if Kirk would just drop them off at one of the stations on Market Street. But Kirk wouldn't hear of it. And judging by the long silences that emanated from the back seat, the ride home wasn't regretted.

Tiffany and Kirk refused a nightcap, and as the couples said good night in front of the Laughlins' buff-colored house, Gina entreated, "Come keep me company Wednesday, Tiffany. It's Tom's poker night. I'll make something Italian and fattening for just the two of us."

"Sounds like an offer I can't resist," Tiffany said with a laugh. "What time do you want me?"

"Sevenish all right?"

"Great. I'll see you then, and bring some wine. Thanks, Gina."

On the way back to the city, Kirk said, "I don't think they're going to have to wait much longer for that baby. Did you like them, Tiffany?"

"Gina's a doll. I don't think anyone could *not* like Gina. She's so honest and down-to-earth and outgoing. But it's hard to like someone who doesn't like you, and I don't think Tom does. Like me, I mean."

"He likes you," Kirk asserted. "He's just overprotective of me—doesn't want me to mess around with bad women." He shot her a humorous glance, but Tiffany ignored it.

"Isn't that a little unusual?"

"You don't know Tom. He was brought up that way— to take care of people. When his dad brought me home and told him to look out for me, right then and there I became his kid brother. He made me go to school every day, and heaven help any guy who picked on me once I got there. Name it and Tom did it for me till I could take care of myself. He's just looking you over, honey, making sure you're good enough for me."

Tiffany saw another beguiling grin coming and turned her head away. "That's something else I wanted to bring up. I think you and your friends are making some unwarranted assumptions."

"That's serious. A policeman has to have a warrant."

"What I'm trying to say, Kirk, is that Tom doesn't have to protect you from *me*. I don't have any designs on you. He told me about that society girl who did you dirt; maybe it's my name that has him confused."

Kirk shook his head. "It isn't that. Tom knows I'm irresistible. He figures if I'm crazy about you, you must feel the same way about me. What bothers him is, are you worthy of me?"

Tiffany looked at his handsome profile. She couldn't see his eyes in the dark, but she was sure they were blue and twinkly. "Something tells me I'm being manipulated."

Kirk raised his hands from the steering wheel. "Not so. Look, both hands are on the wheel. I can drive with *one* hand, though." He lunged toward her, but Tiffany moved away.

"Watch it! I'll make a citizen's arrest if you drive with one hand."

"Of all the citizens I've ever known, Tiffany, you're the one I'd most want to be arrested by. A jug of cheap wine, a loaf of San Francisco sourdough, and thou."

"I thought stale white bread and water was the standard fare."

"I don't know about England where all those corpse-in-the-library mysteries you read take place, but here in California we're updating all the time. What I want to know about is the *thou*." He was braking now in front of The Red Herring.

"The *thou* in question is tired from a very enjoyable evening and thinks she should say good night."

"Without having Davis, Davis, and Davis, the multiple personality architects, advise you on your store layout?"

Tiffany didn't reply immediately. Experts make mistakes. Her bookstore wasn't drawing people as she had expected it would. Kirk Davis's opinion might be helpful.

"That multiple personality doesn't include a Jekyll and Hyde, does it?"

"Just keep your eye on my hands. When they start sprouting fur and claws, call nine-one-one and turn me in."

As Tiffany and Kirk entered the dimly lit store, Kirk flipped all the light switches by the door. When the room was fully illuminated, he said, "What do you think of your lighting?"

Following his glance, Tiffany looked up at the ceiling. It had been the designer's idea to keep the old-fashioned brass gaslight chandeliers that were already in place and wired for electricity.

"Do you fancy flourescent lights here?" Tiffany asked

sarcastically. She glanced pointedly at the walls, wainscoted to chair height with a rich brown walnut, and then at the fine oak floors.

"The light fixtures *look* good, but what do your customers use to read titles by? Candles? Matches?"

"The place is *supposed* to look mysterious, even a little spooky."

Kirk shook his head. "Uh-uh. You're on the wrong track. People don't go to a bookstore to be scared; they go to find a *book* that—maybe—will scare them. All your dim lighting does is make the store depressing, and depressed people don't feel like spending money. They want to get the hell out into the California sunshine."

Tiffany looked around her. "You may be right. The store's gloomy, not mysterious."

An infectious grin flashed across Kirk's expressive face again. "You catch on fast."

"Is there any other advice you wanted to give me?"

"I wonder if your cash register wouldn't be better somewhere else."

Tiffany glanced toward the rear of the store. She had put her cash register at the service desk with the microfiche reader, reference books, copies of *The Red Herring Reader,* and a stack of bookmarks printed with a fat red herring on each.

She was still studying the arrangement when suddenly the store was plunged into utter darkness, and Tiffany screamed. It wasn't a ululating, air-raid-siren type of scream, but a loud high C that began and ended cleanly. What ended it was a pair of wool-clad arms around her and the smell of freshly ironed linen as Kirk drew her against his chest and the handkerchief in his blazer pocket.

"I'm sorry I frightened you," he whispered in her ear, "but I wanted to test your reflexes."

Tiffany pushed violently at him. "Here's one reflex you won't have to wonder about!"

His laugh was low and had a certain note in it that made Tiffany think: *His eyes are turning green!*

"I had to know how good a screamer you are in case

the cat burglar made his way in here."

"In that case, I suppose I could call a cop."

"I understand that they're never around when you want them."

"Too bad that's not true now," Tiffany said tartly.

"Is it really too bad, Tiffany?" The seductive, purring tones of his voice were very close. His breath added its warmth to the heat flooding through her. He caught her face between his palms and tilted it upward. A kiss landed right on the tip of her short, classically straight nose. "I can't see a thing. I'll just have to feel my way," he said, his voice brimming with laughter.

Arrogant! she thought. He'd feel a kick on his ankle— if I could just find his ankle.

But his hands and mouth were doing such marvelous things to her now that anything that would make him stop was out of the question. His long fingers had slid inside her bateau-necked blouse. With his palms flat and warm and hard against her skin, he placed his lips on hers firmly and surely in a kiss that rose to a crescendo like a breaker coming in, then fell to a gentle, slumbrous clinging, only to rise again to a thrilling, towering peak.

When they finally stood apart, Tiffany said, "I want you to turn on the lights."

"Why?" he asked, and she could hear the resistance in his voice.

"I want to check on something."

The lights went on then, and Tiffany smiled triumphantly. "Your eyes are green."

"And yours are brown. And I know a man who has blue eyes. And a girl I used to date had hazel eyes with dark lashes. This is a very interesting conversation, Tiffany. Do you have any other gems of information you'd care to impart to me?"

"Don't you remember I told you that your eyes turn green when you . . . uh . . . feel a certain way?"

"Huh?" Kirk looked at her, puzzled. "You mean the way I feel now?"

Embarrassed, Tiffany nodded.

It was wonderful to see the way Kirk's face lit up. "Oh, now I remember." He threw his head back in a long, delighted laugh. "Beware of the man with green eyes." His eyes narrowed and got that dangerous, prowling look in them again. "Are they still green?" he asked. Tiffany's face gave him the answer. "In that case," he said in a low, smoldering tone, "I'll turn off the lights."

Again the darkness pressed them close together and made everything permissible. Taking Tiffany's face in his hands, Kirk brought his mouth down on hers with unconcealed hunger. Then, delicately, he lifted her short, bow-shaped upper lip with his tongue and caressed its soft underside. Excitement radiated through Tiffany's body like jewel-toned prisms shaken by the wind. Still cradling Tiffany's oval face between his strong hands, Kirk stroked the smooth under part of her full lower lip in the same way. Then, gently, he let his tongue ride the tide of her arousal into the sea-fastness of her warm, eager mouth.

"You're so lovely," he breathed. "So warm and soft and lovely." Holding her close, he pushed her silky hair away from her forehead with his lips and covered its smoothness with kisses. At the same time, he moved the heel of his hand seductively across the thin material that covered her breast, sending hot, licking flames of desire through her.

Tiffany moved against him and felt the promise in every hard line of his body. With one hand, he swept her in even closer. At the same time, his mouth fastened on hers in another long, pulsing kiss while his hand cupped her breast into a voluptuous mound.

Abruptly, she started in his arms and pulled away.

"What is it, Tiffany?"

"Nothing. I heard a noise, that's all. There are mice in the cellar, and I have a thing about mice. I was afraid they might have gotten up here."

Kirk removed one hand from around her and turned on the lights. "Who told you there are mice in the cellar?"

His voice was cool now, his eyes gray, and he released his hold on her.

"Lois Weston, my assistant. She's going to put traps and poison out for them tomorrow."

"How long have you had mice?"

"About two weeks. Why all this interest in the mice? I would have thought stool-pigeons were more your line." Tiffany looked up at him with a mischievous smile. "Get it?"

"Yes." Kirk groaned. "And I love you, anyway."

To her surprise, his expression turned serious and their eyes met and held. What had started as a joke took on a sudden, undeniable reality. Tiffany's heart began to thump painfully. Love was serious. Love wasn't playing around.

It was true that for a long time no man had made her feel the way Kirk Davis did. But it was also true that she could never marry a cop or a fireman or a deep-sea diver or a high-wire artist. She could never again live intimately with another's danger, never deliberately be death's bedfellow again.

Tiffany put her hand in his. "Good night, Kirk. I had a lovely time."

"I'll be in touch." His eyes held her spellbound, and his voice was a caress. "Lock up when I go," he said warningly. "And stay out of the cellar."

Tiffany walked toward the door as he closed it behind him. She locked it securely. What a strange thing to say—"Stay out of the cellar"—when she had already told him she was afraid of mice.

As she went up the stairs to her apartment, Tiffany mused on how quickly Detective Davis, cop, had taken over from Kirk Davis, lover. And there was his third persona—anonymous street person—to consider, too. "Kirk Davis, triple-threat," she said softly and laughed.

That's a lot of man to keep yourself from loving, Tiffany girl!

Chapter   6

TIFFANY WOKE UP the next morning to a nerve-nagging sound that trailed her from the dim reaches of sleep into full consciousness. The aggressive, insistent "meow" was nothing new in Tiffany's life. Her house abutted an alley. However, this cat was closer than that.

She slipped a flower-sprigged peignoir over her nightgown and picked a leather mule off the floor to shoo away the cat with. Then she padded barefoot down the stairs and opened the side door. A large black cat, bullet-slim and sleek, glared at her with malevolent green eyes and meowed commandingly to be let in.

Tiffany let her eyes travel upward. "Good morning, Kirk," she said coolly.

He smiled as though it were after nine o'clock instead of just seven, and he had already had his coffee. Tiffany noted that he was wearing a crisp white shirt and brown figured tie with a brown tweed jacket. Would all that brown make his eyes the same color? Tiffany wondered. She peered through her own sleep-swollen lids. No, his were a clear, affectionate blue this morning. Still, she pulled her peignoir tight around her. They *could* turn green at any moment.

"I was thinking about your store after I left last night." Tiffany looked at him suspiciously. All this boyish enthusiasm was hard to take so early in the morning. "And it occurred to me that a black cat would be just the thing for a mystery bookstore, so I got you one."

Tiffany looked down at the big black cat, whose tail was now lashing back and forth furiously. "Where from—the local coven?"

"It's a nice cat," Kirk protested. He picked the animal up and scratched it behind the right ear. "It'll lend atmosphere to your store and catch your mice, too."

"They're not *my* mice." Tiffany was revolted by the very idea.

"I know, they're Lois Weston's—if they're anybody's," he said in a low key.

Tiffany looked at him curiously, but there was too much going on—the cat and Kirk both on her doorstep—for her to tackle another problem in her caffeineless state.

The cat was purring fortissimo now as Kirk continued to stroke it. "Can't you make her lower her voice?" Tiffany said crossly. "She'll wake the whole neighborhood."

"It's a male cat. And cats don't purr with their vocal chords, as most people think. The sound is a result of a vibration that starts in the chest area and is transmitted to the upper air passages."

"How interesting!" Tiffany started to close the door. "But if you'll excuse me..."

"Are you going to give the cat a good home?"

"I was thinking of a bad home. All kidding aside, Kirk, I don't want a cat. I don't even particularly like cats. Nor do you need to do any more thinking about my store. You may have been right about changing the lighting, but I'll make the rest of the decisions, as I always have, and take responsiblity for them, too."

"Bravo!" Kirk brought his hands together to applaud.

The cat jumped out of his arms and ran past Tiffany through the opened door.

"You did that on purpose!" Tiffany stormed. "You trained that cat to run into my house when my back was turned!"

"I've got to find him," Kirk said urgently, brushing past her. "He's got a nervous stomach, and only the best carpets will do."

Tiffany closed the door and walked slowly into the hall. What good did it do her to play it cool when just a touch in passing jolted her onto some primitive, unwanted plane of longing? Kirk was waiting for her there in the dark hall, and she could tell from the way he looked at her that he had felt the same jolt.

There was no way to hide the curves of her body under the sheer nightgown and diaphanous peignoir, designed to entice by half revealing, half concealing what the nightgown clung to and molded. It had been a gift from a friend whose motive was clear—pretty lingerie leads to romance and the widow Tiffany had grieved long enough. But this was the first time Tiffany had worn it, and she didn't need Sigmund Freud to understand why.

Kirk's eyes shone green and lustrous through half-closed lids. "I could use . . ." He hesitated and Tiffany's foolish heart raced recklessly ahead to meet him. . . . "a cup of coffee."

Tiffany was perversely disappointed, then relieved, then simply mixed up. "So could I!" she said with heartfelt sincerity. Indeed, she knew she needed the coffee more than Kirk who had clearly already had a cup or two. But she didn't feel inclined to challenge him about it.

The cat had gotten to the kitchen before them and meowed accusingly from the corner where a food dish would ordinarily go.

"Will plain milk do?" Tiffany asked on her way to the refrigerator. "Or does he drink only blood?"

"Milk for now. I'll get some cat food later."

Tiffany placed a bowl of milk on the floor. "Good. That way the cat won't be hungry in *your* apartment."

"Don't you like him?" Kirk's woebegone tone made Tiffany look at the cat again. He was clean. He had obviously, judging from his sleek coat, been someone's pet, and there was something satisfying in seeing him lap away at the milk.

"He's all right," Tiffany said grudgingly. "I suppose I *could* try keeping him for one day. It would be kind of cute to have a black cat in a mystery bookstore." A happy smile lit Kirk's lean face. "What's his name, by the way?" Tiffany questioned.

"I don't know. The people at the coffeeshop who gave him to me just called him Blackie."

"I think I can do better than that. How about Edgar Allan for you know who?"

"Poe?" Tiffany nodded, just perceptibly. "Terrific! I knew you'd take Edgar Allan to your heart. Now how about me?"

"I need coffee," Tiffany muttered. She filled the glass carafe with water, poured it into the well of the automatic coffeemaker, then measured out the appropriate amount of ground coffee and flipped the switch. The little red light that came on cheered her immediately. Coffee was on its way. "Breakfast?" she mumbled. "I can give you juice and a toasted English."

"Terrific!" He waggled his brows in a comical leer. "I've always wanted to have breakfast with Tiffany."

"Feel free to drop in any time—on your way to work."

He smiled in that bright, chirpy way of people who have been up for hours and had had all the coffee they wanted. "I'll bet you hate to eat alone."

"I wouldn't bet. Edgar Allan's still slurping up his milk—audibly."

"It shows he feels at home here. I was afraid he might not."

"So was I—with that nervous stomach and all."

With a roar as of water rushing over a dam, the coffee

announced itself perked. Tiffany poured Kirk and herself a cup, and raised hers to her mouth with a silent prayer of thanks. Two swallows and she thought she might get through the day. Half a cup later, she knew it. When she put her cup down, empty, she felt like a new woman, one who mesmerized crowds with her oratory, led corporations to unheard of profits, outwhooped her sister Valkyries with her "Hojotoho!" Now she could handle the juice and English muffins.

When they had finished eating, Kirk said, "I came by early because I have to go out of town for a day or two, and I wanted to introduce Edgar Allan to your cellar so he could get rid of those mice for you."

Tiffany looked alarmed. "I don't want to be there when he does it."

"You won't be. Just show me where it is."

Tiffany debated getting dressed. There was danger in the way Kirk's eyes lingered on her sleep-tousled hair and soft, still-relaxed mouth, then roved in a freewheeling way over her taut, mounding breasts and rounded hips. But he had implied he was in a hurry, so she settled for pulling the loosened peignoir tight again.

The gleam in his now very green eyes told her the effect was probably opposite to what she had intended. So she let the diaphanous garment float around her and said imperiously, "The stairs to the basement are in the hall."

Kirk called to the cat, who was engrossed in licking his paw and passing it over his face to remove the milk from his whiskers. "You look good enough, Edgar Allan. Come on, I've got a job for you to do."

The stairs were narrow and steep. Tiffany held her peignoir up so Kirk wouldn't step on it, and Edgar Allan ran ahead of them. Tiffany stopped on the bottom step. "That's the basement door there. Just open it and go in. I'll go back upstairs. You can let yourself out when you're finished."

Kirk squeezed past her, but this time there was no

control left in either of them. In a flare-up of mutual passion, he caught Tiffany in his arms, and she tipped her face up to his. His mouth descended swiftly, taking her lips with a fierce hunger that left her trembling in his embrace. Then, his need for her still unassuaged, he cascaded a stream of gloriously greedy kisses across her cheek and down her neck.

With sure, skillful hands, he undid the bow that fastened her peignoir and opened it. His glance sped to the deep V of her gown and the lace that made a valentine of her shapely breasts. Tiffany shivered with anticipation at the emerald fire in his eyes.

He plunged both his hands gently under the gown and slipped it halfway off her shoulders. Then he bent his lips to the triangle of shoulder, arm, and breast, and pressed them to the soft flesh, imprinting it with his desire for her. Each kiss was a separate, burning witness to his passion.

His mouth sought hers again. He reconnoitered it with his smooth tongue, stroking her lips persuasively until they parted and her breath met the warm stream of his. Then he made a brief foray into the velvety interior, their tongues meeting in a love-duel. After the raid, his lips engaged hers in a long, ecstatic kiss, while his hands cupped her breasts as though they were precious goblets.

Kirk was holding her so close now that Tiffany could feel the heated strength of his male body. Desire surged through her like a river rushing somewhere to overflow its banks. She moaned softly as he repeatedly passed his hands the length of her with a steady, primitive rhythm like the slow beat of jungle drums.

"You're delectable, Tiffany," he whispered into her ear. "And wonderful," he murmured against the quivering pulse in her throat. "And morning-sweet," he said, closing his mouth over her taut rosy nipple.

Voice-activated like a phone-answering machine, Edgar Allan uttered a piercing meow.

"Shut up, Edgar," Kirk muttered, burying the "Allan"

between Tiffany's full breasts.

The cat responded by rubbing himself against Kirk's trouser leg and purring like a Rolls-Royce.

Tiffany couldn't help herself. She burst into laughter. "He loves you, Kirk."

"That's all I need—a gay cat!"

Tiffany laughed again and, fixing her gown and robe, started up the stairs. "I don't want to be too close when you and Edgar Allan go on your search-and-destroy mission. Just let me know how it turns out."

"Okay. Come on, Edgar Allan, let's see how good a mouser you are." Kirk took a few steps toward the door and turned the knob. Nothing happened. He turned it again, then looked up at Tiffany. "It's locked," he said severely, and she noticed the cold, inquiring look in his gray eyes. He was a cop again, not a lover.

"I didn't know," she faltered.

"Well, where's the key?" Kirk asked in a peremptory voice.

"I don't have one. I never go down there, because I have no reason to. We have plenty of storage space upstairs."

"Well, who does have the key?"

Tiffany resented his impatience, his tone of authority, his whole policemanlike demeanor directed at her.

"The only other person in the store, as you well know, is Lois Weston," she said tartly. "I'll ask her to open the door and leave it unlocked for you. That way, you and your cat can enter any time you want without bothering me."

Another quick change left Tiffany absolutely stunned. Was Kirk a cop or an actor? He was all smiles now, moving away from the door, waving a deprecatory hand at it. "Naw, let it go. Lois probably had a good reason for locking it. To keep the mice inside, maybe. If she's in control of the situation, why should we butt in? I'll just leave Edgar Allan with you for a pet."

"Thanks a lot."

"No problem. Do I have visiting rights?"

"Edgar Allan will be in the bookstore, lending atmosphere, and the store's open to the public." She was still nettled by the quick changes in his behavior and angry at herself for giving way to her own urgent needs.

"Then I'll be seeing you."

Tiffany thought all the colors of his eyes came together then—a flash of green, a bluish twinkle, and a commanding gray. But she couldn't be sure. He had narrowed his eyes as he looked up at her, and besides, it was dark in the stairwell.

Head high, she turned and went up the stairs, her peignoir flowing behind her like a royal cloak. Let him see himself out; he knew the way. But the dignity of her exit was spoiled by Edgar Allan, who seemed to think the floating peignoir was a giant moth he had to pounce on and pin between his coal-black paws. So, holding the royal cloak up around her knees like a washerwoman, Tiffany retreated to her apartment.

An hour before ten o'clock opening time, Lois Weston called. Perhaps it would be better if she didn't come in today. She had a suspicious-looking rash on her chest. It might be a food allergy; on the other hand, Lois had never had chicken pox. What did Tiffany think?

Tiffany thought Lois was probably going to Candlestick Park at one o'clock with a boyfriend, if she had one, to see the San Francisco 49ers play the Atlanta Falcons. But Lois, unlike many applicants for her job, could read and make change, and did show up from time to time. So, fighting back the impulse to say, "I hope you enjoy the game," Tiffany made the by-now stock answer of "I hope you feel better," and hung up.

When Tiffany dressed and went downstairs, she found a sack of cat chow outside the side door—proof that Kirk had been thinking of Edgar Allan, if not of her. Edgar Allan himself displayed a surprising gift for the dramatic. As soon as Tiffany opened the rear door into the bookstore, he leaped ahead of her and made for the highest perch he could find—the top of a bookcase facing the entrance. Glowering with his green cat's eyes, he crouched there all morning. And he was a sensation.

Customers old and new thought he was adorable, that Tiffany was *so* clever to think of a black cat for a mystery bookstore, and swore that they'd have to bring their husbands, wives, fathers, daughters, grand-nephews, to see it. And when they heard that the cat's name was Edgar Allan for you-know-who, they were ebullient and bought lots of mysteries just because they felt so good.

"Good grief, what's that!" Bennett Powell said, as he walked in and the cat hissed at him.

"It's Edgar Allan, and you'd be surprised how much business he's bringing in."

"I don't think that's funny *or* nice, Tiffany." Bennett set his lips in a straight line, and Tiffany was surprised to see how thin and pale they were when arranged like that in his pink beefy face. "Poe was a great writer— the father of the modern detective story, don't forget."

"I won't forget it," Tiffany said meekly. There was no point in arguing. Bennett clung to his opinions like a mussel to a rock. And jokes about the Great Authors were cheap shots. "With all their faults, I don't think any of us could do as well as they did," was one of his favorite rebuttals.

"I thought I'd drop by to see if you wanted to go out tonight. A place on Union Street has got some nice Early American antiques. I was thinking of Mother."

Of course; who else? Immediately, Tiffany reproached herself for the catty thought, but, nevertheless, it was true. If ever a man had been tied to his mother's apron strings, Bennett Powell was that man.

"We could have a bite of supper first, then browse to our hearts' content."

A picture of two velvety brown Jerseys methodically making their way side by side, heads down, through a field of grass and yellow buttercups came into Tiffany's mind. That's what life with Bennett would be like. There'd be no mountains to climb, no torrents to cross, no water-falls to shoot. Just a meadow—and maybe Mother, a somewhat larger Jersey, close behind. A malicious im-age—but, again, an accurate one.

Tiffany swallowed the impulse to say she wasn't in-terested in antiques. Maybe she should have another in-terest. Maybe what she needed instead of Kirk's hot, greedy mouth twisting against hers, his hands stroking her into a state of throbbing, eager delight, his virile body making wanted but unwise promises, was nice, tame Bennett Powell . . . and Mother.

"I'd love to go, Bennett." She glanced toward Edgar Allan, who had tucked his nose under his tail so that he looked like an enormous surrealistic toupee up there on top of the white bookcase. "It's the cat's first night here, but I suppose he'll get along all right."

Bennett hemmed and hawed. "We *could* take him with us."

Tiffany smiled politely. She wondered if something could be done with Bennett. Could he possibly be ren-dered less pompous, even possibly *exciting?* Couldn't you dwell on a man's virtues if you wanted to love him and conversely invent or exaggerate flaws in him if you *didn't* want to fall in love? Bennett had his deficiencies, but she was fond of him; he was good-natured, and they had a love of mysteries in common. Kirk, on the other hand . . .

It didn't work. She couldn't *think* of Kirk Davis, she could only *see* him—those amazing eyes of his and that devastating, devilish grin—and feel his lips and his hands and the hard contours of his body against hers.

But Kirk had his faults, too. When she had time, she'd discover them. She *had* to stop this madness before it went too far. Fall in love with a cop? And an undercover cop, at that! She might as well fall in love with a "jumper" on the Golden Gate bridge.

For her date that night, Tiffany dressed in a demure navy wool suit with a cropped jacket and a white blouse

topped by a ruffled collar. The clothes expressed the way
Bennett made her feel, her "Bennett persona," she called
it. She had bought the suit years ago, even before she
was married.

Bennett's smile of appreciation when he saw her didn't
surprise Tiffany. Bennett liked his women demure.
Mother liked them that way even more.

The restaurant was tea-room style. Everything was
covered with a print fabric, except the plates. It had a
jolly little fireplace, Windsor chairs, and pink-shaded
lamps on each table. The waitresses wore black and white
uniforms, and pleated white cupcakes on their heads. But
the food was surprisingly good.

Tiffany had crab cakes with a remoulade sauce and a
slab of chocolate torte that was a chocoholic's dream
come true. Bennett had a small steak but eschewed the
onions that came with it, and Tiffany deduced that as
usual, Bennett was looking forward—this time to the
good-night kiss that put the seal of approval on their
evenings out together.

On the way to the gallery, Tiffany grew moody. She
knew what lay ahead—dark, shiny portraits of town
worthies in buckled shoes and knee breeches, with white
stockings over thick calves, coats with dinner-plate buttons, and stern, unforgiving expressions; reems of crewel
work done by the worthy's wife and daughters; wooden
carvings of seagulls and roosters and three-masted ships;
and unidentifiable items of kitchen paraphernalia.

"Let's do something different," she said impulsively.
"Go roller-skating, maybe. As an adolescent, I was known
as a fanatic skater in my neighborhood."

"And what would I get Mother for Christmas?" Bennett asked sarcastically. "A pair of roller skates?" Obviously, there was nothing lower than doing one's mother
out of a happy Christmas for the sake of a few hours of
selfish, childish pleasure. But it was Tiffany who finally
found the perfect gift for Mrs. Powell—a pair of Sandwich glass candlesticks, with a slight nick on the base

of one to show it was a genuine antique.

Mollified, Bennett offered to buy Tiffany an ice-cream cone. They walked down the street side by side, Tiffany curling her pink tongue around delicious bits of buried fresh peach, Bennett decorously scooping up spoonfuls of vanilla ice cream from a cup.

"Where did you get that cat?" Bennett asked conversationally, as he dug out the last bit of ice cream. "Has he had a rabies shot? Cats are prone to pneumonitis. What are you going to do about that?"

"Give me time, Bennett," Tiffany wailed. "I just got him this morning."

"He looks like an alley cat. Did you find him on the street?"

Stung by Bennett's contempt for Edgar Allan, Tiffany said, "No, that guy we met on the Sam Spade walk gave him to me."

"You've been seeing *him*—that bum?" Bennett's voice rang with amazement.

"Not *seeing* him," Tiffany said. Just being kissed and held and caressed by him, she thought. "He gave me the cat—to catch mice. That's all."

"How did he know you had mice?" Bennett asked suspiciously.

Tiffany shrugged. "I told him. I wasn't aware that having mice was one of life's unmentionables, like having bad breath."

"If you had told *me*, I would have gotten you an exterminator."

Tiffany fluttered her ice-cream cone vaguely in the air and resisted the impulse to say, "You're not going to tell Mother, are you?"

So far, Bennett had chalked up nothing but zeroes, but he could still redeem himself with his good-night kiss. True, he had kissed her before to no remarkable effect, but at those times Tiffany wasn't trying to fall in love with him.

When Bennett brought her home, Tiffany invited him

in for a nightcap. "Slip into something comfortable like
that chair over there, while I get the makings. White
wine and soda?" she called out from the kitchen.

"Yes, please."

Edgar Allan rubbed himself against Tiffany's legs and
purred like a motorboat. "Oh, Edgar Allan, please don't
trip me up. Go eat your cat chow, and I promise I'll buy
you liver tomorrow."

"Are you talking to that cat?" Bennett had suddenly
appeared in the doorway. "That's a bad sign, Tiffany.
You need a man around the house." He took a few steps
toward her and put his hands on her shoulders. "We get
along awfully well, Tiff. You know that."

Tiffany nodded, but there was an abstracted look in
her eyes. Edgar Allan had bounded away when Bennett
approached and then sprung up onto the windowsill over
the sink, from where he was now staring down at Bennett's slicked-back blond hair in a meditative fashion.
What would happen when Bennett bent his head to kiss
her? As he started to do that very thing, Tiffany warned,
"Bennett, the cat..."

"Forget the cat," Bennett murmured dreamily, his lips
drawing closer to Tiffany's.

But as lips touched lips, Edgar Allan whipped out an
unsheathed paw and batted poor, unsuspecting Bennett's
blond pompadour. Bennett swore and grabbed for the
cat. But Tiffany was faster. She plucked Edgar Allan off
the windowsill and held him in her arms.

"You would have hurt him!" she said, shocked and
angry.

"Not much...I mean, not really. You seem all too
wrapped up in that cat, Tiffany. Can't you put him outside while we have our drinks?"

I know what *that* means, Tiffany thought. Holding
Edgar Allan's comfortable bulk in her arms, she wondered if she wouldn't prefer the animal's company to
Bennett's. But that *would* seem crazy, so she went down
the stairs and put the cat out.

Seemingly happy again with his drink in his hand and

Tiffany beside him on the couch, Bennett said, "You know I'm very fond of you, Tiff, and Mother likes you, too. In fact, you're the only girl I've brought home whom she *has* liked."

"How many girls have you had, Bennett?"

"Oh, not *that* many," Bennett said modestly. He moved closer to Tiffany and put his glass down on the coffee table. "I can't propose to you in Latin the way Lord Peter Wimsey did to Harriet Vane, but I'd like you to start thinking about maybe someday marrying me. Will you, Tiffany?"

"I don't know, Bennett." Tiffany felt a little bewildered. She hadn't been expecting a proposal. Had the fight with Edgar Allan stirred up Bennett's hormones? "Would you mind kissing me first?"

"First?"

"It's a trial by kisses," Tiffany said brightly, "like in the old tournaments. Three men have asked for my hand, and the one who kisses the best wins it."

"You're joking," Bennett said reproachfully.

"Yes, Bennett, I am." Yet Tiffany closed her eyes and leaned toward him, and Bennett kissed her squarely on the lips. I'm feeling something, Tiffany told herself— the beginning of a tiny thrill, just a tingling, really, but it *could* grow. It isn't growing, though. It's dying out. There's nothing there. Bennett doesn't stand a chance. And I'm glad. Because I don't like Mother.

She pulled gently away. "Bennett, dear, I value our friendship very much. Do you think we could leave it that way?"

Bennett was startled but recovered amazingly quickly. "Sure, Tiffany. I understand. I didn't pass the kissing test." He smiled and Tiffany returned his smile. "No hard feelings. We'll always be friends and . . . fellow Followers of the Red Herring. Right?"

Perhaps she had underestimated Bennett, Tiffany mused after he left her. He was a gentleman and a good sport.

A piercing, long drawn-out yowl shattered the night's

calm. Tiffany raced down the stairs and opened the door. Edgar Allan shot into the house with his ears back and his fur raised. He looked remarkably like a cat who had just been kicked.

As she rinsed out the two wineglasses, Tiffany realized how wrong she had been. No amount of dwelling on Bennett's good points could ever have made her fall in love with him. His were not the virtues she craved.

To forestall falling in love with Kirk, she would have to focus on his faults. All's fair if you want peace from love, Tiffany decided, closing the cupboard door firmly on the two glasses.

Tomorrow was Tom Laughlin's poker night, she reminded herself. Maybe Gina would tell her that Kirk had a wife in Daly City and a couple of kids.

Chapter 7

THE NEXT MORNING, Lois showed up contrite and early for work. She wore a turtleneck that practically swallowed her chin. "To hide that horrible rash," she explained to Tiffany.

"How come the basement room is locked?" Tiffany asked.

"Poison!" Lois answered dramatically. "For the mice . . . and possibly rats." Tiffany blanched. "We wouldn't want any of the children who come into the store to get into the basement, would we?" Lois added plaintively.

Tiffany shook her head automatically, too busy blocking the image of big gray rodents with sharp teeth and long slimy tails from her mind to reflect more than fleetingly that children never came into the store without their parents and then only occasionally, and that the basement stairs weren't in the store, anyway.

Still, Tiffany was grateful for Lois's presence, and had her assistant wait on customers while she repriced books she had selected for a markdown sale, entering the date and new price on her stock-control cards.

Tiffany also made a reservation for herself for a weekend stay at the Seacliff Inn on the rugged coast of Mendocino, one hundred miles north of San Francisco. She had already reserved the inn's thirteen rooms for people who wanted to go on the mystery weekend that The Red Herring was arranging. She had also written the script for the "mystery" that would be enacted during that weekend. She now wanted this weekend trip to reacquaint herself with the inn's layout and meet with the actors she had hired to play, respectively, murderer and victim.

The day passed uneventfully. The appearance of Pinky Ring with his brown leather portfolio reminded Tiffany of Lois's writing, and she asked in a friendly way, "How's the book coming along?"

"Slowly. It involves a lot of research. I go to the library practically every night."

Tiffany gave the older woman an appraising glance. From the glow in her skin and the snap in her raisin-black eyes, Lois didn't look as though she spent her nights in a library. Tiffany wondered if Pinky Ring was a love interest, then dismissed the thought. True, he always went to Lois to be waited on, but Lois was probably ten years older than he was. Still, love wasn't always rational ... Tiffany quickly put a damper on such thoughts and concentrated on her job.

When the workday was over, Tiffany changed from the blouse and skirt she wore in the store into a dusty-rose velour leisure suit. She matched it with a pair of pink jogging shoes, scrubbed her face clean of makeup, and applied a rose lipstick. She was ready for a relaxing evening of girl-talk with Gina Laughlin.

To Tiffany's surprise, Gina was rather fussily dressed in a frilly white blouse and a flowing black velveteen skirt. Moreoover, Tom was still home, and the smell that hung in the air was not the tomato-garlic aroma of the promised Italian cooking.

"Corned beef?" Tiffany asked, sniffing.

Gina nodded as she tied an apron around her waist

and led the way into the kitchen. "It's traditional. Corned beef sandwiches at midnight."

Tiffany blinked. Had she come to the wrong party?

"The boys help themselves after the poker game," Gina explained. When Tiffany's mouth made a round pink *O,* Gina said, "Did you think Tom was going-*out* to play poker?"

Tiffany nodded.

"Oh, no, it's our turn to have the guys over. I wanted company because otherwise there's nothing for me to do but watch TV and I always doze off, and then I can't sleep when I go to bed. Besides, I wanted to get to know you better." Gina smiled at Tiffany in her warm, engaging way.

"You'll have to hide me in the kitchen," Tiffany said, laughing and pulling at her velour top. "I thought it would be just us females."

"You look lovely. Kirk will have a hard time keeping his mind on his cards."

"Kirk's coming?" Tiffany stared at the dark-haired woman blankly. First she thought she was going to be alone with Gina. Then she learned the poker game would be there. Now she found out Kirk would be there.

Gina returned her look with surprise. "Of course. He and Tom play poker together every month."

All right, Tiffany told herself, here's your chance. As soon as Kirk walks through the door, look for something to criticize.

The first arrivals, three fellow officers of Tom's, came into the kitchen and were introduced to Tiffany as Chuck, Ron, and Les. They each accepted a beer from Tom, paid Gina a few friendly compliments, and kidded Tiffany about her mystery bookstore.

Tiffany fielded their jokes about The Red Herring with bright, shining eyes and heightened color, but her attention was completely elsewhere. The suspense of waiting for Kirk was filling her with restless excitement.

Yet when she heard his voice at the door, she immediately busied herself with a tray of paper plates, cutlery, napkins, and condiments for the midnight supper.

"How's your cat burglar?" she heard Chuck ask in the dining room, where the men were going to play cards.

"Still lying low," Kirk answered. "I can't collar him till he surfaces again. I haven't even found where he's stashing the stuff or fencing it. But I'll get him. It's just a matter of time."

"Let's play a little poker here," a rough voice that Tiffany recognized as Ron's chimed in. "I don't want to talk shop. I get enough of that garbage all day long."

"Just a minute," Kirk said in a quiet, commanding tone. "I want to say hello to Gina."

Tiffany's heart began to beat painfully fast. No! she scolded herself. Don't let your emotions run away with you like that. Look at him objectively, critically, as just another man.

Kirk stopped short on the threshold of the kitchen. He stared at Tiffany as she stood, slim and straight, her eyes meeting his. His look of surprise shifted instantly into a broad, joyful smile, but underneath Tiffany could see the bone-scraped look of fatigue in his face, the tautness in his muscle set. He looked like a forest firefighter coming in off the line, a battle-scarred soldier, an exhausted cop. He looked intently masculine, and Tiffany felt drawn to him like a woman in a warrior's tent. She wanted to comfort him—to draw his head down on her breast, massage the tension out of his muscles, and love him out of his pain.

"Hello, Tiffany," he said, his eyes blue and happy.

"Kirk," she answered with a little bob of her head.

"Are you going to keep Gina company?"

"Yes. She asked me, remember?"

His eyes locked on hers, Kirk shook his head slowly. "I guess I didn't hear."

This should be taped for "Great Conversations," Tiffany thought. It must be a bad sign when words are just a holding action for what you're saying with your eyes.

I love his lean sun-browned features and tough body. I love the way his face lights up and his eyes change, and the way he orders people around in that quiet manner of his. Dear Lord, isn't there anything about him I *don't* like?

"*Davis!*" came a stentorian yell from the dining room.

"Don't go way," Kirk told her softly, his eyes taking in the rose lipstick, the velour top draped close to her breasts, the pants that clung to her shapely thighs. Even the pink canvas shoes came in for a glance.

"Well!" Gina said, with mock indignation. "I didn't even get a chance to say hello."

Tiffany put the ketchup cover on the jar of horseradish, and the horseradish cover on the jar of mustard, and then stared stupidly at the cover still in her hands, wondering where it had come from. Mumbling into the mustard before screwing *its* cap on, she said, "Kirk's nice, but he's got lots of faults, hasn't he?"

Gina laughed. "Kirk Davis? He's the greatest guy I know next to my Tom. Now that the fellows are settling down to serious poker, what do you say we eat, Tiffany?"

Predictably, Gina's lasagna, made the day before and reheated, was delicious. Tiffany asked for the recipe; but as she savored each forkful, she listened with only half an ear to Gina's litany of ingredients.

The men's voices were clearly audible in the kitchen: "I'm in for a quarter." "A pair of sevens." "Three deuces." "I'll see your bet and raise it a buck."

Tiffany found herself listening for Kirk's clear, resonant tones with their underlay of good humor. And when Ron said, "Hey, Kirk, stop dreaming and deal the cards," Tiffany wondered if Kirk had been thinking of her.

After they had stacked their few supper dishes in the dishwasher, Gina and Tiffany went into the adjoining family room. Gina set to work on the afghan she was crocheting, while Tiffany watched, fascinated by the darkhaired woman's quickness and dexterity.

"I think that's wonderful," Tiffany said, looking down

at her own fingers. "About all I can do with my hands is turn the pages of a book."

"It's relaxing for me," Gina confessed. "And believe me, a psychiatric nurse needs all the relaxation she can get."

"Are you working full-time now?"

Gina shook her head, smiled, and rolled her eyes upward. "Only when the moon is full."

Tiffany laughed, realizing that in the very difficult "caring" professions humor was a buttress against burnout.

"I make practically all my gifts," Gina continued. "I'll probably smother our baby in booties and jackets and blankets."

"He or she will be a lucky child—with you and Tom as the parents."

"I hope so," Gina said simply.

Tiffany looked at her serene companion, the bright orange and beige and brown of the afghan spread over her knees. Tom was in daily danger, yet Gina had no qualms about having a baby.

Gina said tentatively, her voice soft and sympathetic, "I guess you and your husband didn't have time to start a family."

Tiffany's desire to be honest with this woman she liked so much overcame her slight feeling of shame. "I wasn't as brave as you are," she confessed. "My husband had a dangerous job"—Tiffany suppressed the *too*. "He was a wild-animal veterinarian. I kept thinking that someday he'd get out of that line of work, and *then* we'd start raising a family. But he was killed before that could happen."

Neither woman spoke. Tiffany had an idea she knew what Gina was thinking—that because she had no child, Tiffany had been left with nothing of her husband. She had heard that often after Owen's death.

How could she explain to Gina—of all people—that at that time her attitude had seemed right? And that it was academic to say a more mature Tiffany might make a different decision today, inasmuch as she had no intention of ever being in that position again?

Kirk came into the family room just then. His eyes went right to Tiffany. A radiance lit the blue depths of his irises, and his lips curved upward in an infectious smile that made Tiffany smile back.

The house was warm, and Kirk had rolled his sleeves up above his strong biceps and unbuttoned his shirt to a point where a dark, curly pelt showed. His fine-honed features, broad shoulders, well-muscled frame, and the ambience of the men's poker game in the background created an aura of virility that thrilled Tiffany.

"I thought I'd come in and see how the ladies were doing," he said a little shyly.

"Ladies *plural?*" Gina asked. "Quick, Kirk, who am I?"

"Martha Washington." Kirk still hadn't taken his eyes from Tiffany.

"You're right!" Gina answered.

"Davis! You in or out?"

"I'm *in!*" Kirk flashed a grin at Gina. "Keep up the good work, Martha." With a last, lingering look at Tiffany, he turned and went back to the poker game.

"That's one sweet guy," Gina said. "A tough cop, as he should be, but underneath a real pussycat."

Tiffany's heart dropped like an elevator. All the fight against falling in love was oozing out of her.

"You wouldn't be matchmaking, would you, Gina?" she asked humorously.

Gina laughed frankly. *"I* am. Tom's still not sure."

"I'm with Tom," Tiffany muttered, but Gina didn't hear.

As the evening wore on, Tiffany felt a mounting suspense. From the overheard conversation of the poker players and Kirk's frequent trips to the family room, it became obvious that Kirk's attention was more on her than on the game. His ardor fed hers till a provocative sweetness, an edginess of expectation, animated her mind and body.

You'd better get out of here before it's too late, Tiffany warned herself. That's a nine-one-one look in Kirk's eyes if I ever saw one.

She got up and yawned. "I'd better run along, Gina. Tomorrow's a big day, and I still have to get back to the city. Thanks for the supper and the conversation. It's been fun."

Gina put her crocheting aside and rose, too. "I enjoyed it. Let's get together again real soon. I'll see you out."

"Tell Tom and the others I said good night."

"I'll do that."

Tiffany kept her voice low and heard Gina close the door quietly behind her. She went directly to her car and drove off, glad to have made off without seeing Kirk.

As Tiffany drove along, she thought about Gina— her fingers flying in and out as she crocheted, the simple but good meal she had served, the serene confidence with which she looked forward to having a child. Tiffany raised her eyebrows speculatively. She was so different from Gina Laughlin! Tiffany could barely put up a hem, her cooking was cursory, and she was intense and wary about life, not placid. But Tiffany Bradford was the way she was.

With a start of recognition, Tiffany realized that she and Kirk were alike. His fluid, mobile features, the spare, honed-down look of his face, even his way of moving quickly and silently on the balls of his feet—all bespoke the same highly charged nature that she had.

Remembering how he had looked at her, Tiffany felt a warm rush of excitement. He was overwhelmingly masculine and so terribly sure of himself. He had left the poker game often to see her, not caring what his friends said. And how easily he had switched from being a man among men to being a man with a woman. Suppose she had stayed at Gina's—what would have happened between them?

Tiffany straightened up and tightened her hands on the wheel. She had been practically daydreaming and even though traffic on the Bayshore Freeway was unusually light, she shouldn't have let her thoughts wander.

She glanced at her rearview mirror. It was bright with the flashing lights of a police car. Tiffany looked down at her speedometer. She hadn't been speeding. Annoyed with herself, she decided she must have been weaving or driving erratically.

Tiffany pulled over onto the shoulder of the road. While she waited for the cop, she took her driver's license out of her wallet. Then she rolled down her window and sat, staring stonily ahead of her. She might have been in the wrong, but she wasn't going to *plead,* for heaven's sake.

"That was a pretty quick getaway you made, miss." The drawl was unfamiliar, but the voice wasn't.

"Are you *allowed* to do this sort of thing, Officer Davis?"

"If you won't tell, I won't. No kidding, why did you leave without saying good-bye?"

"I didn't want to disturb the poker game."

Kirk laughed. "I wish you had. I left a bundle. The fellas said I must be lucky in love." His voice became softly seductive. "Am I?"

Tiffany's heart was going like a trip-hammer. The surprise of discovering it was Kirk who had stopped her and the excitement of seeing him in this novel situation were unnerving.

Kirk had put on a tan leather jacket, but his shirt was still open to the mild San Francisco autumn night. His lean brown neck was exposed, as was some of his virile chest hair. The expensive leather emphasized the set of his broad shoulders and his narrow waist. His features were hawklike in the dark, his eyes half-hooded as he watched her.

In spite of the smile that played around his finely etched lips, Tiffany felt a flutter of fear. He was the kind of man who got what he wanted, and he wanted her. But she was the one who would have to pay the consequences.

"I wouldn't know," Tiffany said coolly. "What happens now? Am I free to go or are you going to arrest me?" Her voice dripped sarcasm, and Kirk's smile deepened.

"I could arrest you for resisting an officer."

"I'd claim harassment."

"Listen, we can't hang out on this shoulder all night. I'll meet you at your place."

"But I don't *want* you at my place," Tiffany said petulantly.

Kirk's expression grew stern. "Police business," he said gruffly. "I want to check out your store."

"I'll bet!"

"Tsk, tsk." Kirk moved away from the car window, laughing. "What would Lord Peter Wimsey say?"

With the police car on her tail, Tiffany drove at a sedately lawful 55 miles an hour when she really wanted to push the speedometer to 110. She seethed with indignation. How dare Kirk use his position to get his way with her? She'd report him to his superior, go to court and testify against him, see him busted to uniformed status. She fumed and swore and turned the radio on loud as *some* kind of expression of her feelings.

But by the time Tiffany pulled up in front of The Red Herring, the radio was off and she had cooled down. She wasn't sorry to have the store checked before she went to her apartment. The fact that the cat burglar hadn't hit the neighborhood for a while made her uneasy. At least when he struck a business or a residence, you knew where he had been. Now she had the feeling that he was waiting and watching the place he would enter next. And what good fortune ruled that it would not be The Red Herring?

So when Kirk joined her on the sidewalk, Tiffany said, "I'm glad for the presence of your car—if nothing else. It's visible security. Where'd you get it, by the way?"

Kirk grinned. "I borrowed it from Ron. He'll be at that poker game for hours." He started for the side of the house. "Let's go in."

"I thought you were going to check out the store!"

"I can do it better from this side—element of surprise."

Tiffany unlocked the door and entered with Kirk. She turned the lights on and pointed to the door leading into the rear of the store. "There's the store. I'll give you the key, and you can do your thing."

Kirk took her arm and gently propelled her toward the staircase. "I haven't seen you all night," he crooned. "Not really—not to *be* with."

As they moved slowly up the stairs to her apartment, Tiffany's heart pounded with excitement. She had caught a glimpse of Kirk's eyes. There was no doubt about it. *They were turning green.*

Kirk put his hand out for her key and unlocked her door. "I wouldn't have brought you here if I thought there was any danger. There's no one here. I just got a surveillance report from the team that's watching the neighborhood."

"You got me here on false pretenses!" Tiffany's voice rose with anger and shock.

"Right. About as false as any pretenses can be, and I've never met a pretense that wasn't."

"Why?" Tiffany was facing him now, arms akimbo, eyes blazing, daring him to tell another lie.

"I wanted to know why you ran out on me tonight. Have I done something to offend you?"

"You know, you should go out in the neighborhood on Halloween. You're full of tricks and none of them is a treat to me. Now it's the sincerity act, the 'I'm so puzzled' ploy. Well, it won't wash, *flatfoot!*" Tiffany spat out the epithet.

Kirk looked off into the distance. "Let's see," he said thoughtfully, his eyes dancing with laughter. "Mickey Spillane? Chandler?"

"Do you have a home, or do you sleep in the cage in your cop car?"

"I'm not leaving till I get an answer to why you tried to avoid me," Kirk said stubbornly.

"So it's the third degree now, huh?"

"Yeah, right." Kirk pointed to the dim overhead light Tiffany had left on. "Bright lights and everything. Well?"

What could she say? How could she tell him that she was afraid of commitment—and marriage—to a man whose job spelled danger, when he hadn't mentioned commitment, let alone marriage? It was easier to start a relationship than to end one, and if the end looked as problem-filled as this one, it was better not to start.

"Why won't you give a little?" Kirk pleaded. "I don't mean just physically; I mean *you*. I know we have something going. Why hold back?"

The solution suddenly came to her. Time! That was the answer—keep stalling for time. In the end, Kirk would get discouraged and give up. And she would be left with an aching heart but not a desolate one.

"I'll think about it," she said with a smile. She yawned elaborately, her hand over her mouth.

"I understand. You're tired from watching Gina crochet all evening. Will I see you tomorrow?"

"I'm sorry, but I'll be in Mendocino. I have to arrange for a murder."

"Sounds premeditated."

"It is. We have twenty people signed up for a mystery weekend next month at the Seacliff Inn. I've hired professional actors to play the murderer and victim, and I've written the scenario for the murder. All that's left is a final run-through at the scene of the crime."

"How about letting me help? Who knows more about murder than San Francisco's own Sherlock?"

It was a good idea, she realized. With his knowledge, Kirk could be a godsend.

"Separate rooms," Tiffany said warningly.

"Connecting?"

Tiffany shook her head.

"Separate hotels?"

Tiffany laughed in spite of herself.

"Hey, you've got a dimple. Did you know that?"

Tiffany's hand flew to her cheek. She had no dimple! She'd never had one, not even when she was a little girl.

"Not there. Here!"

Taking her hands in his, he pulled her slowly, inexorably toward him, his eyes a beautiful lambent green between narrowed lids. He bent his head and kissed her under the clean line of her chin, spreading his lips a little so that she felt his kiss as a moist, sensuous print.

"Not possible—having dimples there," she breathed brokenly.

"I'm making some for you."

What Kirk was saying was nonsense, but what he was doing was heavenly. His lips were roving the smooth column of her throat, stopping here and there to leave delectable symbols of his desire.

"I don't think . . ." Tiffany started to protest.

"You're right. Don't think," he murmured, his lips pressing the tender hollow at the base of her throat.

"Your kisses are a crime, Detective Davis."

"What you do to me is a crime, Tiffany Bradford." Kirk slid his hands up under her velour top, where there was nothing but her bra between his fingers and her breasts; his fingers soon took care of that. Aching for his caress, her breasts lifted and fell into his hands like ripe fruit.

Kirk closed his green eyes and groaned. He stroked the soft, full mounds with his long fingers, touching just the very surface of her sensitive skin, until her nerves screamed for some kind of completion.

He raised the velour top and had it at her shoulders when a shrill, insistent "meow" drilled through the door.

"It's Edgar Allan," Tiffany whispered.

"I recognize the voice."

Kirk took her lips again, mingling his warm breath

with hers, while he held her breasts cupped in his large, strong hands, as though he wanted to hold them like that forever.

"We have to let him in."

"Why?"

Kirk was fingertipping little circles around her nipples now, then lightly rubbing the pink buds with his palm. Feeling them harden against his hand, Tiffany drew in her breath sharply. The ripples of desire that radiated through her were becoming unbearably tantalizing.

Edgar Allan's meow turned into a plaintive, unending lament.

"He's come home. He expects to be let in. It's unfair to leave him out all night."

"Unfair! Woman, you don't know what *unfair* is."

Tiffany firmly and deliberately removed his hands and smoothed down her velour top. "Will you let Edgar Allan in when you leave, please?" She opened her eyes innocently wide, then had to clamp her small, even teeth on her lower lip to keep from laughing at the expression on Kirk's face.

"Connecting rooms in Mendocino . . . and no cat!"

"I'll see you out," Tiffany said demurely. At the side door, she smiled. "Good night, Kirk. Hi, Edgar Allan. Where have *you* been all night?"

Chapter 8

"YOU *WILL* REMEMBER to mix a little warm water with Edgar Allan's cat food, won't you, Lois, and let him in tonight when you lock up? I don't want him roaming the streets." *Good Lord, I sound like one of those women who lives all alone with a cat!*

"Don't worry, Tiffany. I'll take good care of Edgar Allan."

You asked for it, Tiffany, my girl—the merry little laugh, the knowing twinkle.

"Bennett will feed him and let him out tomorrow morning," Tiffany continued, a little stiffly. "And I'll be back in the afternoon."

The sepulchral melody of The Red Herring's specially designed door chimes sounded.

Kirk entered, and Tiffany thought she had never seen him look so handsome as he did now in a white cable-knit vest over a maroon and taupe striped polo shirt, his arms brawny under the short sleeves, his strong, tanned neck exposed by the unbuttoned shirt. His look of vibrant expectation at the day that lay ahead of them, the way his eyes sought her out, his smile when he saw her, made Tiffany's heart beat absurdly, excitingly fast.

Tiffany wondered if Lois would recognize in this handsome, well-dressed man the street person who had come to Bennett's Sherlock Holmes talk. But it was obvious from Lois's goggle-eyed admiration that she didn't.

As Tiffany introduced the two, she noticed the bland, polite mask that slipped over Kirk's angular features. Only his eyes showed any real expression, and they were gray and watchful, assessing and judging—a policeman's eyes.

"All set?" Kirk asked Tiffany.

With one last look around the store, Tiffany said yes.

When she agreed to make the drive to Mendocino with Kirk instead of by herself, Tiffany had asked that he wait till midmorning and Lois's arrival in the store before starting out. Although Saturday was a fairly busy day in The Red Herring, Lois had assured Tiffany that she would be able to handle the store alone.

So, accepting the fact that she couldn't be in two places at once and that it was essential for her to make this trip to Mendocino, Tiffany handed her weekend case to Kirk, said good-bye to a still wide-eyed Lois, and walked out.

"What did you tell her about us?" Kirk asked.

"Nothing. Just that I was going away for the weekend with a friend. Lois and I aren't intimate. I'm sure she was dying to know more, but there wasn't any more to tell."

Kirk's grin held overtones of that's-what-you-think!

Tiffany ignored the innuendo and bent down to pat Edgar Allan, who was rolling around on the sidewalk, scratching his back on the rough cement.

"So long, Edgar Allan."

The cat meowed a greeting back.

"Hey, Edgar Allan talks!" Kirk said.

"But not to strangers. Not to plumbers, customers,

the paper boy, and so on. Edgar Allan's not very out-going, I'm afraid."

"It's his name," Kirk pointed out. "You shouldn't have called him that."

A gleaming white convertible graced the curb.

"The market went up?" Tiffany asked.

"Not the market. My stocks."

"Maybe you should leave the force and devote your-self full time to finance."

Kirk shook his head emphatically. "Not a chance. I like being a cop." He held the door for her, and when they were both inside, he reached across her to the glove compartment and pulled out a long, feathery green chif-fon scarf. "It'll be windy with the top down, so I got this for you."

A heavy but not unpleasing scent clung to the scarf. "And had it perfumed, too?" Tiffany asked, amused.

"Of course." Kirk grinned at her, a wicked, provok-ing, utterly masculine grin. He watched as Tiffany looked in the rearview mirror and tried unsuccessfully to tie the scarf around her head. "Here, butterfingers." He turned her face squarely to his and expertly wound the scarf around her head, finishing by knotting it securely under her hair.

"Lots of practice, I assume," Tiffany murmured. Jeal-ousy collided with the thrill of knowing that this man who was looking at her with such longing was himself desired by other women.

Then she was rejoicing that it was *her* slim sides his hands were pressing under the light mohair cardigan. And *her* lips that his own were coming down to meet, his green eyes closing, his dark lashes brushing his cheek.

There was a clean, fresh morning taste to his kiss, a soft gentleness that belonged to the start of the day. But just before he released her, his hold tightened. She felt the strength and vital warmth of his hands against her ribs. At the same time, the quick probe of his tongue, thrusting her soft lips apart, bespoke a passion and a promise that fired her senses.

Tiffany moved away from him across the smooth red leather of the seat. "It's not going to be that kind of a weekend, Kirk."

"Even grubby undercover detectives need love," Kirk replied plaintively.

Their way north on State Highway 1 was a continuous postcard of spectacular scenery. To the left, the ocean crashed and banged and lifted itself in towers of spray against cliffs and grass-covered headlands and gaunt black rocks. And on their right, the green and gold tapestry of California—harvested fields and humped-up hills dotted with an occasional spreading oak or clump of sycamores—unfolded.

Then the scenery changed. Pine trees, lighthouses, and little towns of weather-beaten frame houses clustered together on the rocky coast bespoke New England. This was Mendocino County, whose coastal towns had been created as shipping points by the now-defunct lumber industry and whose original settlers had sailed around the Horn from Maine.

The village of Mendocino itself, which jutted out on a promontory over the rocky shore, was a carefully pre-served blend of the gingerbread of century-old Victorian houses with the simplicity of Cape Cod saltboxes and the white spires of New England-style churches. It had become an artists' colony and tourist center, so that bou-tiques, art galleries, and restaurants now occupied build-ings once used by working fishermen and woodsmen. Mendocino's skyline was marked by redwood water tow-ers, weathered to a bleached-out gray, which rose above the gaggle of gift shops as staunchly authentic reminders of the past.

They were ten miles beyond the town when Tiffany pointed to a solitary three-story white frame house on a bluff jutting out over the Pacific. "There it is—the Sea-cliff Inn." Tiffany sighed with satisfaction. "Look at those bay windows and gables and cupolas. Did you ever see such a gorgeous specimen of Victoriana? And just wait till you get inside!"

"Secret passages? Sliding panels?"

"No," Tiffany said positively. "This is not a Halloween haunted-house weekend. Nothing scary or horrifying will take place. The solution of the mystery will depend upon the application of logic. Besides, this is an ordinary Victorian house. It was built in 1879 as a wedding gift for a couple who evidently wanted to be alone together. It was a private residence until just a few years ago, when the couple who bought it converted it into an inn. It has thirteen rooms. That's the only spooky element in it."

"How do they count our 'connecting'—as one room or two?"

"I reserved a single for myself," Tiffany said icily.

"I changed it."

Sparks flew from Tiffany's dark eyes. "I hope not!"

Kirk brought the convertible to a neat stop in front of the door. His silence and his smile were infuriating. If what he said was true, there'd be the devil to pay. Foreign as such behavior was to her, Tiffany wouldn't hesitate even to make a scene if necessary.

However, as she stepped into the parlor of the inn, she realized that no place was less conducive to raised voices and angry words than this. The red Turkish carpet, Tiffany lamps, bric-a-brac cabinets, and maidenhair ferns in brass pots—all demanded gentility.

Therefore, Tiffany said nothing about her room to the young woman who registered her and Kirk at a pine desk in a cubbyhole off the parlor. She decided to adopt a wait-and-see attitude as, Kirk behind her, she followed the porter who carried the bags up a steep, narrow staircase and watched him unlock first one and then an adjoining white-painted door. She entered her room and tried the lock on the connecting door. It worked. Kirk was hardly likely to batter the door down.

Tiffany took off her cardigan and stood a moment,

relishing the coziness of the room. A brass bed covered with a flowered quilt stood against one wall, which was papered in a matching print. A marble-topped dresser, red plush Victorian chairs, and a small fireplace occupied the others.

She listened to the rhythmic boom of the ocean, then stepped out on the balcony to fill her lungs with sea air. She noted with distaste that the rear of the house had been modernized. Each room opened onto a long, continuous balcony, where opaque Fiberglas dividers provided privacy.

When she reentered her room, the connecting door was open, and Kirk was lounging against the doorjamb, hands in his pockets, a silent whistle on his lips.

Tiffany glanced pointedly toward the open door. "How did that come about?" she asked coldly.

Kirk held up a small piece of wire. "I learned lock-picking from some of the best."

"I take it this is a demonstration of what you could do anytime you wanted to."

"But wouldn't."

"What does that mean?"

Kirk tossed the wire into the wastebasket. His eyes prowled the silky mass of her brown hair and the column of white throat exposed by the tangerine silk shirt that draped and outlined and clung to her proud, upthrust breasts. "I'll wait for an invitation." His eyes narrowed to glints of green between half-closed lids, and he smiled with maddening assurance.

A flush of excitement suffused Tiffany's body. She compressed her lips against it and arched her brows haughtily. "Gilt-edged?"

"Guilt?" Kirk said, purposely misunderstanding. His eyes swept the room. "Something tells me this is the wrong setting."

"I'll stage a murder in a Vegas hotel next time," Tiffany said sweetly. "In the meantime, how about a nice, brisk walk on the cliff?"

Kirk cast a last, regretful look at the brass bed. "I'll get a sweater." He went into his room. Tiffany formed the words, "Knock next time!" in her mind but didn't say them. She'd leave it up to him not to enter except at her invitation—an invitation that, in spite of the mating call her body was making to his, she would never give him.

Tiffany grabbed her cardigan off a chair and stepped to the threshold of his room. "I'm ready," she said breathlessly, as though she had come a great distance.

"You didn't knock."

"Shall I go back and do it again?" she asked sarcastically. Throwing her sweater across one shoulder, she folded her arms across her chest and faced him with flashing eyes. Anger was her defense against the desire that was bringing her to crucible pitch.

"I don't think you wanted to knock." His voice was low and vibrant with meaning. He went to her and gently unwound her arms, dropping her cardigan to the floor and brushing her soft breasts with his hands. "You're like a pretzel," he murmured. "All tied up in knots."

What had been her own arms across her breasts became his hands, stroking and caressing the full, aroused mounds. His lips stayed on hers, too, seeking and tasting until their bodies relaxed and began to blend. Then his kisses became wilder. He swept her into him and fastened his mouth on hers, capturing it in quick, hungry movements, taking all of it again and again till she felt weak with a wild, barbaric fever.

"Tiffany! Oh, Lord, how I want you."

His hot, excited breath fed her passion. Her lips parted eagerly under the onslaughts of his, and his warm, velvety tongue glided smoothly into her mouth. His sensitive hands stroked her sides and back in long, thrilling sweeps, then dropped to her buttocks and thighs, and molded her close to him. She trembled, and with a feverish moan he brought her even closer, till their bodies were locked together.

Swept away by rapture, Tiffany nibbled at Kirk's cheek, tasting the roughness of it between her lips. Then she darted her tongue like a hummingbird's into his ear. She pulled his polo shirt out from his pants and eased her hands up under the shirt. Laying her palms flat against his stomach, she felt his muscles tense up under his smooth skin. All the while, she thought she would melt under the emerald fire of his eyes.

"I'm crazy about you, Tiffany," he breathed hoarsely. "Crazy, wild!" He put his face under her fluffy hair and nibbled at her earlobe just sharply enough to send a spear of unalloyed longing stabbing through her. Then he trailed his lips down her neck and nuzzled the soft flesh of her shoulder, making her quiver with the keenness of her pleasure.

Tiffany's hands went to her blouse. She laughed. "I don't want you ripping the buttons off with your teeth."

"I told you I was wild about you." His hands covered hers, and he slipped the small shell buttons out of the buttonholes with tantalizing slowness, his fingers brushing the silk of her blouse erotically against the sensitive flesh underneath. He slid the blouse off her shoulders and gazed with reverent wonder at the first rise of her creamy breast under the lace-trimmed bra. Then he bent his lips to the soft flesh and mapped a blue vein with kisses at the same time that his hands slowly pushed down the straps of her lingerie.

She stood revealed then in her feminine glory. Throwing back her head, Tiffany exulted in the look she had aroused in his eyes. They were a smoldering green now, as he took in the long line of her white throat and her ripe, young breasts.

"Tiffany... my own beautiful, gorgeous Tiffany."

Then all talking stopped as he poured out his love in a storm of kisses. It was as though he had to kiss every part of her or lose her. His lips swept over her neck and her breasts, searing her with their passion, branding her as his own. Tiffany linked her hands behind his neck and arched her back, offering herself to him. She felt his hands, firm on her buttocks, keeping her pressed close to him. His growing hardness matched her own state of arousal. Fervently, she slipped her hands under his polo shirt again and spread her fingers over his firm flesh.

"My brass bed or yours?" he whispered.

"Mine is too far," Tiffany murmured.

From then until they were in bed, Tiffany had no memory of what transpired. The room was a confused blur of garments flying through the air. Her skirt and his pants dropped to the floor. Socks, shoes, and underwear lay together in a heap of castoffs.

Leaning over her, Kirk said huskily, "Tiffany, you're beautiful."

"Just a woman," she answered modestly.

"But what a woman!"

He kissed her with a tenderness that made her desire him with exquisite urgency. Every part of her wanted to possess him. She took him to herself in every way she could, pulling him down on her with her arms tight around his neck, opening her mouth for his moist, probing kiss, touching him all over with a sense of awe that this was indeed he, and they were truly together.

Then she lay quiet as his mouth plundered her sweet places, making them throb with desire and expectation. She whimpered with longing as Kirk led her up a staircase where every step—every touch and kiss and caress—was an unbearable crescendo.

Finally, there could be no more waiting for either of them. A tremendous sigh escaped Tiffany as he entered her. She could feel him inside her, and outside, as he slid his hands beneath her hips, locking her body more tightly to his. Her entire world was Kirk—his thrusting strength, and the narrow hips that she gripped, and his loving mouth fastened on hers. Then it was more. It was a terrible, rending rapture that exploded into an ecstasy neither of them had ever known before.

When they returned together to the world they knew,

their entwined bodies shiny with sweat, they lay in a hush of wonder, trembling in the afterglow. Gradually, their breathing slowed and their hearts began to beat normally. They released each other then into a serene embrace.

"Marry me, Tiffany," Kirk said hoarsely. "I don't want an affair. I want to be your husband. I want you to be my wife."

"Isn't it too soon?"

"Lord Peter Wimsey proposed to Harriet Vane the first time he met her."

"You read *Strong Poison!*" Pleased and surprised, Tiffany sat up in bed.

"I had to, for the sake of my work. We get a lot of aristocratic cases in the Tenderloin." He reached up for her and, his hands on her bare waist, pulled her down beside him again. He folded his arms around her and kissed her tenderly on her temple and the bridge of her nose and the corner where her full lower lip curved upward. "Lord Peter *is* my only rival, isn't he? You're not stuck on that guy Powell?"

"Bennett's just a friend, and I love you even more than I love Lord Peter."

"Glad to hear it. I was worried there for a minute. So?" He began to stroke her breast with the back of his hand. Its fine hairs lightly grazing the surface of her skin sent ripples of pleasure through Tiffany again.

"If you do that, I won't be able to say no."

"Why do you think I'm doing it?"

Tiffany laughed and took his hands in hers, holding them tight. Her expression turned serious, and her voice became small and uncertain. "You wouldn't think of changing jobs, would you?"

"No, Tiffany," Kirk said with finality. "And you wouldn't really want me to." He dropped her hands and turned over on his back. "I know you're afraid of marrying a cop, but other women manage. Look at Gina."

"I'm not Gina," she said, suddenly bitter at his refusal

to recognize her individuality and to give her fear the respect it deserved.

"I'm sorry, Tiffany. That wasn't fair." He raised himself on one elbow and looked down into her face, his eyes warmly blue with love. "It's just that knowing as many cops and cops' wives as I do, it's hard for me always to understand how you feel. Sometimes I think it's a coverup, that deep down inside you don't really love me, and that's why you refuse to marry me."

"I love you, Kirk. You can believe that."

His features sharpened with desire, and his eyes turned predatory. The tender, smiling blue left them. They were the green of one of the big cats now, hunting at night.

His mouth came down hard on hers. At the same time, he swept his hand over her breast, curving his fingers around the swell of it. He stroked her flat stomach and let his fingers trail till they touched the now-throbbing heart of her desire.

Tiffany began to breathe heavily. Her body arched under his hand. Her lips clung to his, as though all of life was contained in his breath. "You're being unfair again," she murmured when he finally lifted his mouth from hers.

"All's fair in love and war," Kirk muttered, his green eyes heavy with desire.

This time, he asserted his love in ways that left her senses reeling, showing her the kind of man he was, insisting that she recognize it. And Tiffany did. She pleaded with him to end the exquisite anguish he was putting her through. She moaned with her need for completion. When it came, she drowned as he carried her, their nude bodies pressed each to each, down to the bottom of a green, white-sanded sea.

Finally, spent and replete, she surfaced, and found herself lying in his arms, saying, "Yes, I will marry you."

But Kirk had fallen asleep and didn't hear her. Tiffany looked into his face. How necessary the familiar geometry of that straight nose and finely etched mouth had become to her. What would she do if, having found him, she ever lost him? A chill washed over her and she trembled in his arms. Kirk tightened his hold on her and smiled in his sleep. And Tiffany lay there, rigid with anxiety, and whispered, "No. I'll love you like this, but I'll never, never marry you."

Chapter 9

"WHAT'S IT DOING out there?" Tiffany stretched luxuriously and pulled the flowered quilt up to her chin.

Kirk turned toward her from the window. He had donned a bright blue terry-cloth kimono wrap and belted it loosely around his waist. Its white shawl collar came to a deep V just above his navel and it stopped at midthigh. His eyes sparkled and a happy grin lit his face. "It's a great day for a murder... or making love."

"That's the most subjective weather report I've ever heard."

Kirk drew the curtain aside and looked out the window again. "Okay, will you buy gray clouds, angry sea, and pine trees twisting in the wind?"

Tiffany shivered. "I'll buy a warm bed." She glanced toward the fireplace. "And a fire."

"And a warm man?" Kirk asked suggestively.

Tiffany looked at his strong legs covered with dark hair. "My warm man's got gooseflesh."

"*Somebody's* got to let the cat out, take in the morning paper, and light the furnace," Kirk said in a martyred tone. He moved to the fireplace and put a long match to the paper and kindling that had already been laid on the grate. When it caught, he put a log on, dusted his hands, and crawled into the big brass bed beside Tiffany.

"Oh, you poor darling, your feet are like ice! What you don't do for me. Here, I'll warm them." Tiffany took his long, bony feet between her slender ones and slowly rubbed the cold out of them.

"Umm," Kirk said contentedly. "Let's move up here after we're married and I'll light the furnace every morning."

"Are your feet warm?"

"Yes, but the rest of me isn't." He put his arms around her and pulled her toward him. The terry cloth of his robe was rough against her bare skin. Then it was gone, and there was nothing but his silky flesh against hers, and his mouth blowing soft kisses all over her, and his eyes shining green in the firelight.

The contrast between his early-morning, boyish look and mature maleness set up an excited thudding in Tiffany's pulse. His mouth tasted warm from sleep, and as his tongue glided lazily between her lips, Tiffany closed her eyes and thought it was wonderful to loaf at making love, to feel his mouth loiter on hers, to stretch indolently under his caressing hands.

Slowly, as if savoring each movement, he began to stroke her, running his hand from her shoulders to her delicately curved hipbone. Then up her thighs in long, sensuous sweeps to the throbbing delta between.

His mouth followed the trail his hand had made. His tongue dallied with each rosy nipple, caressing it, drawing a moist, sensuous arc around it, then—like a magic wand—flicking it into life. When it hardened between his lips, he groaned with satisfaction and continued his lazy kisses, imprinting every curve and hollow of her with the dewy warmth of his lips.

Dreamily, Tiffany sat up and pressed Kirk gently onto his back. She ran little tongue kisses around his ear, then dropped her lips to the strong cords of his tanned neck.

She buried her face in the thick woolly pelt on his chest and teased his male nipples with quick little tugs of her teeth. Slowly, she kissed her way down to Kirk's hard, flat stomach and stabbed playfully at his navel with her pink tongue.

"Tiffany!" Kirk groaned. "My wild, wonderful Tiffany." He pulled her down on top of him and helped her adjust her body to his. Stroking the straight line of her spine and caressing her rounded buttocks, he eased her into a smooth, slow rhythm. Then he brought his hands around to her love-swollen breasts and kneaded them till Tiffany trembled with the poignancy of her arousal.

The exquisitely pulsing, incredibly erotic movements of their lovemaking made Tiffany feel that she was in an Arabian Nights palace of paradisiacal delights. Then the meter quickened. Tiffany's hips began a more rapid motion, and Kirk arched upward, his hands on her waist, to meet her. In a delirium of rapturous excitement, Tiffany lowered her head to Kirk's and parted her lips for his tongue's smooth, caressing entrance into the moist warmth of her mouth. Suddenly, there was nothing in the whole world but the primeval thrusting rhythm and the fiery rise to a sharp, strobe-lit instant of final, piercing rapture.

Afterward, feeling blissful and complete, Tiffany lay in Kirk's arms and languidly watched the orange flames sport in the fireplace. Kirk leaned over her and kissed her tenderly, then searched her eyes with his own. "I love you, Tiffany, and I'm asking you again. Marry me, so we can love each other for the rest of our lives." His eyes suddenly sparkled with fun. "I assume you're not looking for just a gigolo."

Tiffany laughed, a happy, burbling sound. "I don't think I could afford you. Who taught you how to play the market, anyway?"

"I taught myself—did a lot of reading and took a couple of classes in investing." Kirk laughed shortly. "I thought my prospective father-in-law would like a rich cop better than a poor one. So you see, with that extra income, we'll be able to travel, eat in the best restaurants, have a good time when we're married."

His eyes watched her narrowly, and they were a cool sea-gray now.

"Is this a test?"

"Yes."

Tiffany sat up and pulled the quilt around her so that only her bare shoulders and the swell of her breasts showed. "Then I'm flunking it," she said quietly. "I can't answer now. I need time."

Kirk sat up, too. He looked sardonically at the floral wallpaper and old-fashioned furniture. "Women used to hold out for marriage," he said ironically. "Now they hold out for affairs."

"I'm not holding out for anything, Kirk Davis. I'm a businesswoman with appointments to keep. I'm getting up." She threw the covers off and jumped out of bed. Cold, in spite of the fire, she grabbed Kirk's robe off the top of the bed and wrapped it around her.

His eyes flicked over her lazily. "That looks better on you than on me."

Ignoring him, she went to the connecting door and turned the knob. The door remained shut. "It's locked. I'm locked out of my own room!"

"Then I guess you'll just have to stay in mine." Kirk's voice was a blend of seductiveness and barely contained amusement.

Tiffany gave him a dirty look and went to the door that led to the hall.

"It's nine o'clock, Tiffany. There'll be lots of people going downstairs to breakfast."

Tiffany wheeled around and went to the balcony door.

"Not the balcony! It's dangerous."

"Sure. One flight up."

Tiffany walked out onto the balcony and examined the divider between Kirk's space and hers. The Fiberglas went almost but not quite all the way to the railing. It would be a piece of cake to get into her room. She squeezed past the divider and turned the handle of her door. Nothing gave. This door was locked, too.

Disappointed, she stood and thought a moment. She remembered the sign by the reception desk—CONTINENTAL BREAKFAST SERVED SUNDAYS FROM EIGHT TO TEN— and Kirk's remark that everyone would be going to breakfast now, at nine o'clock.

Why not try it? Tiffany thought. If her plan didn't work, Kirk was a police officer. He could get her out of any trouble she might get into.

So she squeezed past another divider and peered into the room that lay to the right of hers. Clothes were scattered about on the twin beds, and the room was empty. Tiffany tried the door. The handle turned easily, and she stepped inside.

She heard a man's voice, then a woman's answering him—the man in the bathroom, the woman in the walkin closet. Tiffany hesitated. Why hadn't she thought of that? But no matter, three long steps and she'd be out the door, unobserved.

"Hey! Stop! Hold it right there!"

It was the man—short, rotund, bald—emerging from the bathroom with a medicine bottle in his hand.

"What is it, Franky duck?" Tiffany caught the note of alarm in the trilling voice. The woman, a birdlike, middle-aged blonde, stepped out of the closet and did a double-take when she saw Tiffany. She glared at her husband. "A friend of yours?"

"I must apologize," Tiffany began.

"I should think *so*," the wife interrupted. "How about you, Frank? Do you care to join in this little apology?"

"I locked myself out of my room," Tiffany said firmly. "I didn't want to go through the corridor. It's crowded at this hour." Her voice faltered. What she was saying, under that pale blue gimlet eye, didn't make much sense.

"You locked yourself out of your room *where?*" the woman asked. Her eyes flicked over Kirk's oversized, ankle-length kimono. The wide sleeves hung like pillow-cases, and Tiffany had tied the belt around her waist twice. Wifey cocked her ear dramatically toward the balcony door, which rattled noisily with the wind from the sea.

"I was on the balcony. I love a storm-swept sea. Don't you?" Tiffany looked at Ducky, but that was a mistake. He shrank back against the wall and cast a fearful glance toward his wife. Suddenly, he jumped, and Tiffany started, too. Wifey had just clapped her hands together.

"What are we thinking of, just standing here!" she said. "Frank, search the room! If any of my jewelry is missing..."

As Frank unglued himself from the woodwork, a single sharp rap sounded at the door. "Police! Open up!" The classic words were Kirk's, and Tiffany closed her eyes in unspoken gratitude.

Wifey looked triumphantly at Tiffany. She even said, "Aha!"

Supported by authority, Ducky became a lion. "Stay here! Watch her!" he barked. "She's probably got the stuff stashed in her pockets."

He scuttled to the door while Tiffany looked, be-mused, down at Kirk's robe. What pockets? She could have hid the crown jewels of England up the kimono sleeves, if she'd had a way of keeping them there.

Then her heart leaped up with gladness. Kirk was there, neatly dressed in a blue short-sleeved cotton sports shirt with a button-down collar, his navy sweater dash-ingly knotted around his neck. He looked the very picture of authority, his lean features definite and sharp, his gray eyes coldly commanding.

"Kirk! Never again will I say, 'You can't find a cop when you need one.' These people..."

Reaching into his pocket and flashing his plastic iden-tification card, Kirk interrupted Tiffany. "Is this the woman?" he asked the couple.

"Yes, Officer!" Wifey and Ducky squawked in uni-son.

"She was in here going through the bureau drawer where I put my jewelry," the woman frothed in a torrent of accusation. "Search her! You'll find a short string of pearls—very good—and a long string—not so good—and other pieces that some people might call costume jewelry but that are absolutely irreplaceable and very valuable for sentimental reasons, and . . ."

Tiffany put her hands to her ears. "Kirk! Will you stop her please and let me get out of here! I explained to them that I entered their room by mistake, and frankly I can't stand much more of this nonsense."

"You'll have to come with me, miss," Kirk said solemnly, putting a hand on Tiffany's arm. "Quietly, I hope. We don't want to disturb the other guests." His other hand went to his trousers pocket. "If you don't come quietly, I'll have to use the cuffs."

Tiffany was too shocked to speak at first. Then she whispered hoarsely, "Kirk! Don't do this to me."

Kirk ignored her. "If we find any of your property, ma'am, I'll let you know and rest assured you'll get it back."

"I insist that she look in her bureau drawer this instant," Tiffany said. "I won't budge till she does." She planted her feet squarely on the floor and stood like that, Kirk's restraining hand on her arm.

Kirk nodded, and Wifey went to her marble-topped dresser. She opened the top drawer and pulled out a long double strand of cheap-looking artificial pearls.

"Keep going!" Tiffany commanded.

A heap of junk jewelery came next.

Tiffany wrenched her arm out of Kirk's grasp. "The P.D. will hear about this. I'll have you up on charges of false arrest."

"I'm afraid you'll still have to come with me, miss."

Tiffany stared at him. Had he lost his mind? What the hell was the matter with him?

"Why, for heaven's sake?"

"A little matter of illegal entry, miss."

"Stop talking like somebody from Scotland Yard,"

Tiffany screamed. She searched her mind for an epithet that would express her frustration, shock, and anger. "Pig!"

"She's vicious," Wifey said, a mixture of sorrow and horror in her thin, reedy voice. "She needs help, Officer. The sooner the better."

The hint didn't hang in the air long.

"I'm taking her with me, ma'am, don't worry." Kirk put his hand on Tiffany's arm again. "Come along now, miss, and no trouble, please."

"Yes, Sergeant Cribb," Tiffany hissed. "Just wait till I get you alone."

His face grave, his eyes sad, Kirk ostentatiously tapped his head as he led Tiffany out. As the door closed behind them, she heard Wifey say, "I know I should feel sorry for her, but..." And Ducky, "What do you think she meant—'when I get you alone'?"

Tiffany's room was only a few steps away. Kirk used his plastic ID card to unlock the door, and Tiffany strode in. She ripped the robe off and threw it at Kirk. Then she grabbed the quilt off the bed and wrapped herself in it.

"Get out!" she yelled, firing the words at him like bullets. "I never want to see you again. Do you understand?"

Standing facing her, he was openly laughing now, his eyes a sparkling blue. "I got you out of their room, didn't I?"

"I was on my way out when you walked in," Tiffany retorted.

Kirk shook his head slowly. "She would have hid her junk jewelry, claimed it was good stuff, and tried to pin theft on you for the insurance."

Tiffany could only stare at him, round-eyed. "How do you know?"

"When I saw you enter the room, I listened at the door and figured that was her game. And her husband would have gone along with the scam. Or maybe would have tried to blackmail you into something else. Did you see the way he was looking at you?"

Tiffany shuddered. "Don't remind me." She searched Kirk's cheerful face with her eyes. "Should I be thanking you then?"

His lingering glance stripped the guilt from her. "Certain forms of gratitude are always welcome."

"Don't bother explaining." She peered at the big sports watch on his wrist. "Now, if you'll excuse me, Officer, I'd like to shower and change. A killer and his victim are waiting for me in the parlor."

"Knock on my door when you're ready, and we'll go down to breakfast together."

"What happens if we meet Wifey and Ducky?"

"The pair next door?" Kirk asked with a grin. "They're checking out."

"How do you know?"

"Elementary, my dear Tiffany. I saw an open suitcase in the room, and a piece of tissue paper had wrapped itself around Wifey's heel. From which I conclude that she was packing to leave."

"A marvelous piece of logic, my dear Sherlock, but why should I knock on the connecting door when you can just pick my lock and walk in?"

"Gentlemen lock-pickers never work before noon."

Tiffany lowered her lashes and smiled. Kirk could make her furious and he could make her laugh. He excited her and troubled her as no one else ever had. Her life suddenly seemed rich, intense, superabundant. Love was a wonderful state to be in. But would it last? Could she trust a man with changeable eyes?

Tiffany chose a red turtleneck sweater and a charcoal-gray corduroy jumpsuit to wear for the day. The jumpsuit was belted and had chest pockets that buttoned over a flap. She unbuttoned the suit to the waist and pushed up the sleeves so that the scarlet sweater showed underneath. Sassy red earrings and red espadrilles completed the ensemble.

The sweep of glossy brown hair down past her right

ear and part of her cheek lent the right touch of allure. Her skin glowed with the excitement of love. She applied just enough makeup to give her face a finished, smooth look. Then she knocked on the connecting door.

"Umm. You're lucky I didn't *break* the door down." Kirk reached down for a kiss, but Tiffany deftly stepped away, into his room.

"I need my breakfast," she said firmly. She closed the door behind her so it locked and, followed by Kirk, left the room.

When they entered the inn's parlor, Tiffany whispered to Kirk, "There's my murderer—that dreamboat with the chocolate eyes and melting smile. I'm treating him and the victim to three square meals, gas money from San Francisco, and rehearsal pay for the day."

As Tiffany advanced toward the outstretched hand of Race Prescott, she looked around for the other actor. Tiffany knew Race, whose real name was Roy Potter, from her meals at the Carrotstick Café, where he waited table, peeled vegetables, and bussed dishes while waiting for Hollywood or even San Fran's own American Conservatory Theatre to call.

Race had leaped at the chance to do a little acting for actual cash-in-the-palm recompense. He had given Tiffany a carob cookie and an extra bag of caffeine-free herbal tea without charging her. He had also promised to provide a partner, another actor who would portray the victim—or the murderer, if it turned out that way. But where was the victim? Unless . . .

Even as Tiffany greeted the actor and introduced the two men, her eyes drifted to the frail blonde sitting next to Race. The young woman had drenched violet eyes, a soft, vulnerable mouth, and just the right number of freckles powdering a perfect, suspiciously surgeon-molded nose.

"This is Cheryl," Race said. "She'll be your victim."

Cheryl opened her eyes wide as Limoges saucers, and her lower lip trembled a little. "There won't be any blood, will there? I can't do blood."

"No, no blood," Tiffany stammered, her thinking stalled by so much tremulous emotion.

"Or violence of any kind? I can't stand violence." This time Tiffany was sure Kirk had snickered.

"There has to be *some* violence," Tiffany explained. "I mean, you do end up dead."

As Cheryl bit her lower lip with her pearly teeth and twisted her pale hands in distress, Race whispered to Tiffany, "She needs the money. Her room rent's due."

Thinking to reassure Cheryl about her role, Tiffany said cheerfully, "Kirk is a detective. He'll help us with some of the details of the murder."

"A *real* detective?" Cheryl's sculptured lips formed a silent *O*.

She's apt to get murdered for real if she acts like that during the mystery weekend, Tiffany mused. Race looks as if he wishes he had paid her room rent and left her home. And what's my Kirk doing?

Tiffany glanced at Kirk. She particularly wanted to see his eyes. But all she caught was the tail end of a smile as he turned his head away.

"One of San Fran's Finest," he said amiably.

"I think we should have breakfast," Tiffany announced, her voice crisp and dry.

Race helped Cheryl to her feet as though she were made of china and might break without his assistance. Then they all sauntered into the dining room.

By this time, breakfast had given way to the inn's popular Sunday brunch. However, a canceled reservation got the foursome a table right away, close to the cobblestoned fireplace. Once they all sat down, their glasses were immediately filled with champagne. All except Tiffany's, which she turned stem up. "It's a little early for me. I'll stick to coffee."

"Champagne is all I ever drink." Cheryl's silvery, musical tones rang out from her corner of the room. "I find that coffee muddies the complexion. It has to, don't you think? It *looks* like mud."

All eyes swiveled from the dark brown liquid the waiter was pouring into Tiffany's cup to Tiffany's face. Maybe I'll kill her myself, Tiffany thought darkly. That way, I'll save the price of an actor as well.

A buffet table, resplendent with an ice carving of a dolphin, two tall vases filled with yellow and white chrysanthemums, and platters of cold meat, cheeses, and salads occupied one wall, and was adjoined by a table of hot foods and a baron of beef on a carving stand.

"May I get you something from the buffet table, Cheryl?" Kirk asked.

"Arsenic," Tiffany muttered.

"What did you say, Tiffany? Race has been telling me how brainy you are, and I'd just hate to miss any of your *bons mots*." Even her French is good, Tiffany groaned inwardly. "Though I may never get to be a *very* big star, I'll always appreciate what drama school did for my diction," Cheryl said. "Nobody *ever* has to ask me to repeat what I've said."

Race got up then. "I'll get your food, Cheryl. What do you want?"

"Just a slice of lemon and a glass of hot water, please."

Tiffany glanced in disbelief at the lavishly laden buffet table and then at Race. How would he take this minimalist request?

"One slice of lemon, one glass of hot water, coming right up."

"If nobody minds," Tiffany said heavily, "I'll get *my* breakfast now."

Tiffany's pain at Kirk's neglect of her was even stronger than her amusement at Cheryl's blatant tactics. Looking down at the array of salads before her, she didn't know whether to drown her sorrows in food or take advantage of her unhappiness and lose a little weight. The sight of Race carrying a thin yellow crescent of lemon on a plate and a glass of water decided her. *Somebody* had to get his money's worth out of this brunch.

"You're going to eat all *that?*" Cheryl said, when Tiffany placed her heaped-up plate on the table.

"That's only the salad course."

"Do you have a good exercise program?" Cheryl asked with sincere interest. "You know, much of the body mass in older women is fat."

"Aren't you going to get *your* breakfast, Kirk?" Tiffany asked pointedly.

He tore his eyes from Cheryl—eyes, Tiffany was glad to see, that were not *yet* green, anyway—and said absently, "Yes, of course."

After brunch, the four went to a small games room adjoining the parlor and spread out on one of the felt-topped tables a copy of the building plans that the owner of the Seacliff Inn had given Tiffany. With one break for lunch, they spent the entire day tracing with a grease pencil the comings and goings of the "mystery" group and making changes, when necessary, in Tiffany's script.

Kirk's interest in Cheryl was obvious. He sought her opinion, looked at her constantly, and once, Tiffany noticed, actually started when Cheryl touched him. The young actress responded to Kirk's attentiveness like Pavlov's dog to the ding-dong of the dinner bell. She gazed up into Kirk's face with eyes so wide, she looked like a street waif staring into a bakery window. Cheryl hung on Kirk's every word, and once she realized the effect her touch had on him, her hand impulsively flew to his again and again as she nodded in cloyingly sincere agreement.

Tiffany pictured herself as having a heart with an enormous crack down the middle, like a broken heart on a valentine, and had a definite pain in her chest to go with it. She was shocked by the quick change in Kirk's feelings and humiliated by his obvious preference for the young actress. Most of all, though, she felt the desolation of loss. She had fallen in love with Kirk.

Was that the reason for his interest in Cheryl? Tiffany asked herself. Was he trying to make her jealous so that she would realize she loved him? With a wry face, Tiffany discounted that possibility. Women liked this line of reasoning, but in her experience it rarely motivated men.

As the afternoon wore on, Cheryl's smarmy winsomeness began to sandpaper Tiffany's nerves. Moreover, the pieces of broken heart in the valentine had come together and were emitting flashing red danger signals. Instead of feeling sorry for herself, Tiffany was becoming fighting mad. It wasn't a matter of fighting for her man. She didn't *want* any man who could fall for a dish like Cheryl Scott.

But she had a responsibility to the twenty people who had paid to come to the Seacliff Inn for a smoothly executed mystery weekend. The victim was supposed to be a mousy librarian, not the femme fatale Cheryl was shaping up as. Without credibility, there could be no interest, and Tiffany's customers wouldn't get their money's worth. So the pain in her chest transferred itself to another part of her anatomy, and its name was Cheryl Scott.

When Cheryl went to the ladies' room and Kirk went off in search of a newspaper, Tiffany leaned across the table and looked Race squarely in the eye. "I don't care if your girl friend's room rent is due. I don't think she's right for the part. She's also phenomenally stupid. I mean, even in acting, I don't think one takes pot shots at one's employer the way she's been doing at me."

Race lowered his head sheepishly. "That's my fault. I told her you were a very nice person, and Cheryl took advantage. She's like that. She's got to grab off all the men before someone else does. She thought you were too nice to hit back."

"She's your girl friend and she acts like that?" Tiffany asked, amazed.

The young man shrugged. "We have an open relationship. In the end, we always come back to each other."

"How good an actress is she? Obviously, I don't need

a Tony Award winner for this little production, but I do
need someone who'll show up and who'll learn her lines."

"Cheryl's a pro like me," Race said proudly. "She'll
come through for you. I wouldn't have recommended
her otherwise."

That takes care of the acting end, Tiffany thought,
but how about Cheryl's behavior? Various solutions passed
through Tiffany's mind. She could fire the actress, but
then all the preparations would have to be made with
someone else. She could talk to Cheryl, but the girl
seemed the type who didn't have much control over her
yen for men. Tiffany knew she could unsheathe her claws
and try to match Cheryl in cattiness, but she wasn't very
good at that, and losing would be disastrous.

Cheryl was on her way back from the women's room,
freshly made up and dewy looking. Kirk caught up to
the ingenue and they entered the room together. Idly,
Tiffany's mind began to play with a thought. If Cheryl
was as good an actress as Race said, why couldn't she . . .

"I was just thinking," Tiffany said as Kirk held Cheryl's chair for her. "Why couldn't *you* play the murderer,
Cheryl?"

"The murderer?" Cheryl's hand flew to her heart. Race
opened his sleepy eyes. And Kirk listened with obviously
keen interest to what Tiffany was saying.

"I think it would work . . . be better, even." Tiffany
was genuinely excited now, her mind racing with ideas.
"You're a recluse. We'll give you the attic room. The
guests see you just once—when they arrive. No one
suspects you of the murder because you seem too delicate
and ethereal"—Cheryl brightened at that—"but you're
also a frump. You *can* do something with your hair to
make it dingy, can't you?" Tiffany asked, looking owl-
eyed at Cheryl. "And find unattractive clothes—even
worse than the mousy librarian getup?"

With a wary look in her eye, Cheryl said yes, she
thought she could.

"But of course if you don't want to do this . . ."

"It's all right," Cheryl said in a flat monotone. "The money's the same?"

Tiffany nodded.

"Who'll be the victim?"

"Race."

"Why would a recluse murder a mousy male librarian?" Cheryl asked contemptuously.

"She knows that he's found the papers proving he's the heir of Cheney House, which is what the family home is called. She's afraid he'll put her out once he inherits the house, so she kills him."

"And just how does this recluse murder the librarian?" Cheryl's tone was sarcastic.

"Poison," Tiffany informed her. "She slips it into his bedtime toddy and cuts the bell rope by which he tries to call the servants."

"That'll mean learning a bunch of new lines."

"You can do it, Cheryl. I told Tiffany what a good actress you are." Race flashed a signal with his eyes that Tiffany interpreted as, If you want a roof over your head say yes.

"Okay," Cheryl said, resigned. "When do I start being a recluse?"

"Right now," Tiffany said sweetly. "Go to your room and take this with you." She handed Cheryl the building plans. "Figure out how you'll get from the attic room to the victim's bedroom without being seen. I'll come up shortly and give you the new lines to learn. It won't take me long to write them."

Tiffany rose. Fighting back a look of triumph, she said simply, "I'm going to my room to do the rewriting. We'll go over it again later."

She swept out, her mind teased by the unfathomable look in Kirk's eyes. What did it mean? What did he really think of her? Of Cheryl Scott? Never mind a mystery weekend at Cheney House, Tiffany thought. There were enough mysteries right here and now at the Seacliff Inn. What with a kooky actress, her laid-back boyfriend, and a detective with the morals of Sam Spade.

Tiffany slammed her door shut, wedged a small, plush-covered Victorian side chair under the doorknob of the connecting door, and seated herself at the dainty desk in her room. She worked rapidly, redrafting scenes and dialogue. There was no sound from the room next to hers. Once in a while, she raised her head and chewed on her pencil. Where was he? The only answer Tiffany could think of—the only *logical* answer, she told herself—was Cheryl's room. Tiffany bent to her yellow lined pad again and with angry jabs of her pencil added to the murderess's description, "has a large, hairy mole on her right cheek."

Chapter 10

A SINGLE QUICK knock at the connecting door brought Tiffany to her feet. Still absorbed in her script, she opened the door without thinking. Kirk stood there. He had changed into a blue velour jogging suit.

"I want to see you," he said urgently.

"The feeling's not mutual. I'm busy. If you'll excuse me." She started to close the door, but he put his foot in the way. "An old cop trick?"

Kirk grinned. "So's this." He squeezed his broad shoulders through the narrow opening and took a long step into the room.

"Shouldn't you have a search warrant?" Tiffany said sarcastically.

"This is purely social." The grin held—a devastatingly handsome slash of white across his lean, tanned features. "I want to talk to you." His voice was quietly insistent.

"And what you want, you get, of course, by virtue of the authority that's in you."

"Whatever that means." He was openly amused now. "Look, the weather's cleared. There's a sunset. When was the last time you were out of this mausoleum?" He looked pointedly at the old-fashioned furniture.

"Yesterday," she admitted ruefully.

"Let's go," Kirk commanded, starting for the door.

Tiffany hesitated. "I've got work to do—the script. You heard me; I'm supposed to give it to Cheryl today."

He turned around and came close to her. Looking into her eyes, he said seriously, "There's trouble between us. If we don't do something about it, it'll fester and get worse. That's more important than the script. I . . ."

Whatever he was going to say was lost as she brushed past him, past the arms that were reaching out for her, past the intense bluish-green eyes. "Let's go for that walk," she said brusquely.

When they stepped outside the hotel, Tiffany threw her head back and closed her eyes for a moment. After a day indoors, the air was heavenly—brisk and clear, but not cold.

She had decided on a sophisticated attitude toward Kirk's flirtation with Cheryl. She would be friendly but not loving. She would accent what was positive in their relationship and ignore what was negative. For example, she would enjoy this striding along on the cliff beside Kirk now, head high, arms swinging, and convince herself that the enormous lump in her throat was just a postnasal drip.

The grass under their feet was rough and coarse and springy. The sky was brushed with colors from apricot to a scarlet like flamingos' wings. And the sea held the quiet of approaching evening, slapping at the black rocks near the shore almost playfully, not tearing at them as though to uproot and destroy.

"I wanted to explain to you about Cheryl," Kirk said quietly.

"You don't have to explain anything to *me*. A toss in a brass bed doesn't mean you've got a brass ring through your nose. I'm not your keeper."

"Yes, you are, and I'm yours."

"Oh?" Tiffany's voice rang all the changes on disbelief. "Why?"

"Because we love each other, that's why."

"Really! And what did you have in mind—a *ménage à trois,* consisting of you and me and sweet Cheryl?"

"If I seemed to be paying too much attention to Cheryl," he continued stubbornly, "it's because she fascinated me."

"A common complaint, I believe."

"I was looking for someone."

"Most people are," Tiffany retorted. But Kirk's low, quiet tones and thoughtful expression were nudging her into serious attention to what he was saying. "Did you find her?" she asked.

"Not *her*. I was looking for *myself* as I was ten years ago when I was in love with Roberta Perrin, the girl whose family I worked for as a security guard. She and Cheryl have the same quality of vulnerability. In Cheryl's case, it's put on; in Bobbie's, it wasn't.

"Bobbie really was vulnerable. She had been so sheltered from life by her parents that she was actually innocent, like a child. But like a child, when she didn't get her way, she could go into the most godawful tantrums you ever saw in a person ostensibly grown-up. All day, I've been wondering—what was I like then? How could I have loved Bobbie, when I love you?"

"What happened to you and Bobbie?"

"I fell out of love with her. I hate to say it. For a long time, I even felt guilty about it, because she needed me. I was the one who kept trying to make her grow up. She might have made it with me. But"—Kirk shook his head sadly—"I just didn't love her anymore. It's hard to love a twenty-year-old infant. The honest thing was to tell her, and I did."

"Tom says that she was a spoiled brat and that her family fired you and wouldn't give you a reference."

"That was afterward." Kirk made a wry face. "They weren't crazy about having me as a son-in-law, but they would have accepted it. What they couldn't take was the insult when I broke the engagement. And it's not true that Bobbie was just a spoiled brat. Tom tends to see things in black and white. She *had* potential. It just couldn't go anywhere in that environment."

"What happened to her?"

"Nothing drastic. She married soon after. Someone from a wealthy old family. How happy she is, I don't know." They walked along in silence for a while till Kirk asked boyishly, "Were you really jealous of Cheryl?"

"Not at all! I was contemptuous of you for liking her."

"Yeah, right." He shot a sidelong grin her way.

"I'm going back to my room, Kirk. I really do want to finish that script," she said stiffly, not quite ready to make up yet.

"Wait a minute. Look at this place. It's perfect for a murder."

Tiffany stopped short. "It is, isn't it?"

They stood side by side, looking out to sea. "No witnesses," Kirk said. "Just a couple of cormorants out on the rocks and that pelican skimming the surface for fish."

Tiffany shivered. "You're not developing homicidal tendencies, are you, Detective Davis?"

"Tendencies, yes, but not homicidal."

Gently, he drew her into his arms. "Remember that marriage proposal I made?"

"I remember." She looked up into his face, then turned her head away, abashed by the tenderness she saw there.

"I'm promising you a lifetime of bliss. Here, let me give you a sample."

Putting his finger under her chin, he turned her face back to him. His eyes were a pale green in the setting sun and his face was bronzed by it. His lips were warm and pulsing with life. He took her mouth again and again, twisting his own against it and kissing away the pout that lingered on her full, prettily curved lips.

"I have to go back, Kirk," she said finally, breaking away.

"That's all right, hon. I have a whole suitcase of samples I can show you later."

Arms around each other's waists, Kirk and Tiffany walked back to the inn.

Race was waiting for them in the parlor. "I was hoping you'd get back soon. Cheryl and I have to start back to the city. Do you have that new script for us, Tiffany? We know the layout of the place now and we plan to rehearse together, so I don't think we'll have any problem with the changes."

"It could stand another reading, but under the circumstances, I'll get to it right away."

When Tiffany returned from her room with the script in her hand, she paused on the threshold of the parlor. Cheryl and Race were standing close to each other, talking, while Kirk idly leafed through a magazine on the coffee table. And now it was Race who was drowning in those smoky violet eyes.

Tiffany handed the script and a check to Race. "That's for both of you. Any questions, please call me at The Red Herring. Otherwise, I'll see you both here on the date we agreed on."

Tiffany looked directly at Cheryl. A knowing look passed between the two women. It acknowledged that Cheryl had made a power play and lost. Now the actress knew what she had to know to keep her job—that Tiffany was the boss.

"So now what do we do for kicks?" Kirk said when Race and Cheryl left.

"Go back to the city ourselves. It's a fairly long drive."

"No more brassiness in bed?"

"Definitely not!"

The day after their return to San Francisco, Kirk called. "How about dinner tonight? It's going to be foggy. Very mysterious," he added in a deep voice. "Bring Edgar Allan. We'll introduce him to the Hound of the Baskervilles."

"I've got a better idea. Why don't you come to The Red Herring and address the group? The speaker of the evening can't come. You can tell them what it's like to be a real-life detective."

"Can't," Kirk answered laconically. "It would blow my cover. Besides, I'll be busy. The cat burglar struck while we were away."

"Really? Where?"

"That posh antique store two streets down from you. He walked off with a valuable little statue, and I don't mean the Maltese Falcon."

"You didn't blow your cover with Lois," Tiffany argued.

"Even so, I'm not going to get in front of an audience in the bookstore. If tonight's out, how about tomorrow?"

"Love to," Tiffany answered.

"I'll let you know the time later."

"All right."

Tiffany hung up and immediately dialed Bennett's apartment. Fortunately, Bennett was home and knew someone who would be delighted to address the Followers and who always had material ready.

Tiffany discovered that evening that Bennett's find was a forensic odontologist who proceeded with merry enthusiasm to regale his audience with descriptions of the many cases in which he had identified victims and assailants alike by bite marks and dental work.

"Don't grit your teeth," Bennett said to Tiffany midway through the dentist's lecture, "but isn't that your friend the bum?"

With that absurd little leap her heart always gave when she knew she'd see Kirk, Tiffany followed Bennett's gaze. For a moment, she thought he was wrong—that some street person, not Kirk, had wandered in and sat down.

The long, straight hair of Kirk's wig was pulled back in a ponytail under a visored baseball cap. It looked greasy and unwashed. His eyes were sunken and his face unshaved. A stained bandage rode one cheekbone.

Tiffany pursed her lips in a silent whistle. She would have had a hard time recognizing in this dirty, mean-looking city tough the man who had made love to her.

"It looks like him," Tiffany said carelessly.

"Aren't you going over to say hello?" Bennett taunted.

Tiffany knew that Kirk had seen her looking at him, but he gave no sign of recognition. She let her gaze travel back to Bennett with studied casualness. "Don't be a fool, Bennett. He might have attached himself to me on that Sam Spade walk, but he certainly isn't a friend."

"Do you want me to get him out of here?" Bennett flexed his big shoulders longingly.

Tiffany shrugged. "He's not doing any harm."

"I'll leave him alone if you say so, but how about going somewhere for a bite after the meeting?"

Tiffany had to clap her hand over her mouth to keep from laughing. "In light of tonight's talk, could you rephrase that invitation, please?"

Bennett smiled, but as Tiffany said yes, she wondered if Bennett's invitation wasn't a mild form of blackmail. If she had said no, would he have tried to oust Kirk?

When the lecture was over, they drove to a suburban shopping mall and one of Bennett's favorite eateries—a yogurt parlor with white wrought-iron furniture and fluorescent lights that turned skin the color of skimmed milk.

"A sandwich, Tiffany? They grow their own alfalfa sprouts here."

Tiffany's gaze traveled automatically upward to the ceiling forested with hanging green plants. "I think just a frozen yogurt, thanks."

"What kind? They've got vanilla, chocolate, strawberry, eggnog, and peanut butter today."

"Peanut butter, I guess."

"What kind of topping? Carob sprinkles, yogurt chips, roasted trail mix, honey-apple granola?"

"You pick it," Tiffany said, suddenly depressed. She

missed Kirk with an overwhelming feeling of loneliness.
She didn't want to be in this too-bright place with blond,
bland, yogurt-loving Bennett Powell. She wanted to be
in some dim bar holding hands with Sam Spade's heir,
her own dark, saturnine detective, Kirk Davis, gazing
into his eyes, watching them turn green with desire for
her.

Between spoonfuls of eggnog yogurt topped with carob
sunflower seeds, Bennett unrolled for Tiffany his thesis
that the pipe Sherlock Holmes most liked to smoke was
not made of clay, as most of his admirers thought, but
was a briar pipe.

Tiffany listened only enough to put in a "Yes" and "I
see" at the appropriate places. Her mind was on Kirk.
For the first time, it occurred to her that he might be in
immediate danger.

So far there had been no violence during the neighborhood robberies, but that didn't mean violence couldn't
occur. It was even conceivable that the burglaries were
the work of a gang, not an individual. And who would
be more vulnerable in that case than an undercover cop
who had gotten wind of something?

Tiffany's throat constricted with fear so that even the
yogurt refused to slide down. You're overreacting, she
told herself sternly. But had she been overreacting when
she kissed Owen good-bye every morning with fear in
her heart until the phone had rung with the message she
knew she would one day receive?

Wrenching her mind away from the morbid theme,
Tiffany turned her full attention to what Bennett was
saying. But it was no use. Sherlock Holmes's pipe lost
out in the contest with thoughts of Kirk.

Only this time, Tiffany didn't see him in the ragged
jacket and sandals of his undercover role. In fact, he
wore no clothes at all. Instead, his strong, graceful body
was wrapped around hers in the big brass bed. His green
eyes made love to her. Then his gentle hands touched
her all over, kindling her senses till she cried with her

need for the passionate force of him surging through her body.

When Tiffany got home and said good night to Bennett, she looked for Kirk. But Edgar Allan was the only one there to greet her. She picked up the big black cat and scratched him behind the proffered right ear. As he purred with contentment, Tiffany laid her face against his clean, thick fur.

"What'll I do, Edgar Allan? I love him terribly and I'm worried about him. I can't think about anything else." The cat placed a soft paw on Tiffany's hand. "Thanks for the consolation, pal. Who said a dog was man's best friend?"

Tiffany's fears for Kirk disappeared in the light of day. If anything had happened to him, Gina or Tom would have told her. No news was good news, and the best thing for an attack of jitters was to get away. She would leave Lois alone in the store and get a badly needed haircut, go to the bank, do a little shopping, and have lunch with Ruth Engle, a friend and former classmate who taught at Berkeley.

Tiffany put on a smart red suit as a morale-builder, and to go with the crisp day, then backed her car, an old VW that had trained on San Francisco's hills, out of the narrow garage. She drew up beside a patrol car stopped at a light and compulsively looked over at the two cops inside. Because of Kirk, she was fascinated by policemen now. Then she quickly averted her eyes before they could catch her looking at them.

But as the light turned green, and Tiffany shifted gears and started forward, both men smiled broadly and waved. Disconcerted—did she know them?—Tiffany smiled back. They stayed in her rearview mirror for a good two city blocks, still smiling and, when they caught her glance, waving again. She would have to describe them to Kirk, Tiffany decided, or kid him about San Fran's friendly police force.

Tiffany had to wait for her haircut and wait at the bank, too. She bought a pair of shoes, then hurried to make her luncheon date in Berkeley. As she threaded her car adroitly through the heavy noontime traffic, she passed the same patrol car. At least it seemed to be the same, since the cops smiled and waved again.

Once out on the freeway, she was able to pick up speed. When she saw a motorcycle cop behind her, she frowned with annoyance. She wasn't going any faster than anyone else. Why pick on her? If necessary, she thought with a recovery of good humor, she'd tell this khaki-clad, gold-helmeted state cop about her friends in the patrol car.

But to Tiffany's relief, the highway cop didn't pull her over. He drew up alongside her, grinned and waved, and roared past. Tiffany sketched a feeble wave in response. What was going on? Had Kirk been talking about her to every cop in California?

Tiffany lingered over lunch with Ruth, enjoying every minute of this holiday she had given herself—the glass of Chardonnay with the excellent crab Louis, the interesting nautical displays in the restaurant, a locally popular seafood place, and the easy, intimate conversation. It was fun to be frivolous for a day—to do nothing more serious than wave at some cops and get a haircut and gossip about what so-and-so was doing now.

Then Ruth looked at her watch. "Heavens, it's ten to and I've got a class at two. Let's pay and run."

As they stood at Tiffany's car, there was time for only a quick good-bye and a vow to do it again soon. Ruth passed in back of the VW as Tiffany went around to the driver's side. Tiffany heard a hoot of laughter and turned around. Red-faced and laughing, Ruth called to her and pointed to the rear of the VW. Tiffany walked slowly back, suspicion—but of what, she didn't know—building in her mind.

A bumper sticker—large and clear, black letters on white—adorned her car. CUDDLE UP TO A COP, it said.

Tiffany closed her eyes and gulped. She felt herself turn red instantly like a boiled lobster. "How will I get home?" she moaned. "Every cop in the city waved to me on the way out here."

"When I think we wasted time talking about *other* people," Ruth said, still burbling with laughter. "Who is he?"

"He's a detective who does undercover work in the city."

"Undercover?" Ruth gave her a wide-eyed, amused look. "Well, I should think so!" And she bounced away.

Tiffany glanced at her own watch. She had promised Lois she would return at two-thirty. There wouldn't be time to get the bumper sticker off. So she started back, speeding a little. What cop would give her a ticket with a message like that on her bumper?

This time, a little grin lurked under the artificial smile she returned to San Fran's waving Finest. It was outrageous of Kirk to have done that, but it was funny, too.

Then the old worry came back. Kirk must have put the sticker on her car last night when he was hanging around the neighborhood. She hadn't seen him today. Had anything happened to him?

Chapter 11

SMALL AS THE VW was, the garage behind The Red Herring fit it like a glove. Tiffany got out of the car and looked at the bumper sticker again. She really should remove it, or at least cover it up. But, narrowing her eyes in a secret little smile, she decided not to—for a while, at least. It was an amusing reminder of Kirk.

Not that she needed a reminder. As soon as Lois left, Tiffany called Kirk. She heard the phone ring in his apartment and waited, hoping that he was in the shower or that he would walk in and pick up the phone. But the repeated ringing was the only sound in the emptiness. Nor did anyone answer the phone at the Laughlins' house.

The afternoon wore on to its close with just enough customers to keep Tiffany mildly busy. But the worry within her mounted. This is the way it would be if you married him, she warned herself. What difference would marriage make? the answering voice within argued. You're sick with worry about him now.

At six o'clock, with The Red Herring empty of customers, Tiffany locked the front door, hung the CLOSED sign out, and called Edgar Allan. The big black cat leaped gracefully down from his self-appointed perch on the bookcase and bounded ahead of her up the staircase to her private apartment.

Tiffany opened a can of veal slices in gravy, spooned some out into a bowl, added warm water, which was the way Edgar Allan insisted on having his food, and slid a frozen dinner into the toaster oven for herself.

Why didn't Kirk call? In a kind of frenzy, Tiffany dialed first his number, then the Laughlins', over and over, until the oven timer buzzed. She glanced down at Edgar Allan, who was staring disconsolately into his bowl of veal slices.

"Try it, Edgar Allan," Tiffany urged. "I know it's a new flavor, but how can you tell you don't like it, if you don't taste it?"

The cat flicked his tail back and forth disdainfully, then turned and stalked into the living room. Tiffany could hear him clawing spitefully at the couch but didn't stop him. Where was Kirk? If he was safe, why hadn't he called?

Tiffany sat brooding over her three-hundred calorie dinner. Maybe she should exchange meals with Edgar Allan. The veal slices in gravy looked more appetizing than her chicken dish.

Finally picking up her fork to eat, Tiffany visualized the raucous crowds of North Beach, the bright lights of Chinatown, the coziness of Gina's family room, the brass bed, and Kirk's arms around her. Her eyes glistened with self-pity. All that was needed to complete the picture, "Lonely Woman with Cat and TV Dinner," was a bottle of wine.

She had that, too, but she wasn't going to open it. You don't come through two years of widowhood without character.

It was the sudden dearth, Tiffany thought. Being with Kirk and having his love had made loneliness unbearable now. If I married him, there would be no more loneliness, she mused. We would be like Gina and Tom. Tom has been on the force for years and nothing has happened to him. And Gina was planning a baby soon.

Tiffany ate half of the three-hundred calorie dinner and scraped one hundred-fifty calories into the garbage disposal. That left a credit of one hundred-fifty calories, so she decided to have wine after all and poured herself a glass. She chose a recently published mystery to read and lit the gas grate. Then she curled up in a chair and intermittently read and watched the blue flames leap and fall in the fireplace. Edgar Allan stationed himself nearby on the rug, paws tucked under him, eyes closed, looking like a polished black statue of a cat.

Tiffany looked up from her book. "All we need is a raven tapping on our door and quothing 'Nevermore,' Edgar Allan."

The sudden loud rap on the downstairs door sent Tiffany into instant panic. Halfway down the stairs, she called out a quavering, "Who's there?"

"The police, sweetheart. Open up," Kirk answered in a Bogart lisp.

Tiffany sped to the door, with Edgar Allan leaping ahead of her. Kirk was there, handsome and debonair in a tan sports coat, khaki chino slacks, and a white cotton dress shirt with a blue and white diagonally striped tie.

"Oh, Kirk!" Tiffany said breathlessly. "I've been *so* worried about you."

"Have you?" His voice was suddenly boyish. "That's the best news I've heard all day—and let me tell you, it's been a long one. Hi, Edgar Allan." Kirk bent down and scratched behind the cat's right ear, while Edgar Allan meowed a welcome. "See, he even turns his head so I get the right one," Kirk said. "How about you? Which ear do you want scratched?" He moved toward her, but Tiffany laughed teasingly and started up the stairs, with Kirk behind her.

Kirk made a show of looking around the living room. "Aha! A cat, a fire, a book, and a glass of wine. What does that tell us, my dear Watson? A beautiful young woman is alone for the evening and misses her lover very much."

"How do you deduce that, Sherlock?"

"You have central heating, so obviously the fire is for cheeriness; the cat for company; the book for culture, to which single women tend to be addicted; and the wine for . . . ahem, solitary conviviality."

"And the lover?"

Kirk's voice dropped to a low seductive tone. "That's a given. I saw your face when you opened the door." He advanced toward her again, and again Tiffany moved away.

"I had quite a day, being smiled and waved at by all the cops in town."

Kirk grinned. "That's a cute bumper sticker, isn't it? As soon as I saw it, I thought of you."

"Thanks," Tiffany said dryly.

"Well, are you?"

"Am I what?"

"Are you going to cuddle up to a cop—this one, in particular?"

This time, with a half-smile on her face, she stood still while Kirk took one long step toward her and folded her in his arms. He nuzzled her neck and said huskily, "I've thought of you all day and of coming home to you like this."

She *was* his home, Tiffany reflected, as he was hers. Home had nothing to do with place; it was where the heart lived.

So Tiffany wound her arms around Kirk's neck and whispered, her breath warm on his lips. "You're home, darling. Home in my arms."

"You'll marry me, then. Make it permanent."

Tiffany bent her head. She wanted to bargain, to ask him please to consider changing professions. But that was emotional blackmail, and she wouldn't resort to it. Instead, she thought again of Gina and Tom and their baby to come. If Gina can do it, so can I, Tiffany told herself.

Kirk put his finger under Tiffany's chin and lifted it so he could look at her, blue-green eyes to brown eyes. "Hey, that was a marriage proposal, not a challenge to go six rounds in the ring. What were you thinking of?"

Tiffany was determined not to have the slightest hint of a secret between them. "Of Gina and what a good cop's wife she is."

Kirk looked away, his face suddenly weary. "Tiffany, you can walk out on Geary Street and get killed by a falling brick or a car that goes out of control or almost anything."

"Some jobs are more dangerous than others," Tiffany said softly, willing herself to bring her fear out into the open, to lay it before him so he would know her in all her weakness.

"The people doing those jobs don't think about the danger overmuch, or they couldn't perform. And neither do their wives. They learn together to accept the dangers." He raised her face to his again. "Think you'll be able to hack it?" His voice was gentle, his eyes faintly amused. Then his look grew stern and his voice rasped in his throat. "If not, as much as I love you, I want you to say no."

All her love for him rose in a swelling tide of faith. Nothing could harm two people who loved as they did. "I'm not afraid, Kirk. I want to marry you."

"Oh, Tiffany!" He swept her into his arms and rained insatiable, wildly hungry kisses on her lips and cheeks and throat. He possessed her with his kisses, drawing her to him until she was breathless with delight and felt no will but his. She was still clinging to him, half-swooning with passion, when he murmured against her love-bruised lips, "We'll have to celebrate."

"Mendocino's awfully far."

"I didn't think you slept on a bookshelf like Edgar Allan." He brushed her lips with his once again. "That's an invitation," he whispered wickedly. He took her hand and said, "Come," and she led him into her bedroom.

"Turn on the light," Kirk said. "I want to see you."

Tiffany turned on a pink-shaded lamp that she kept on a table by the door for its rosy, welcoming glow when she entered her room.

She took Kirk's face between her two soft hands.

"What are you looking for, Tiffany?"

"The color of your eyes." She laughed, a rich, delighted chuckle. "I suppose it gives a woman a kind of advantage—to love a man with color-coded eyes. She always knows where she is with him."

"What color do you want them to be now?" Kirk asked huskily.

"Guess!" She nibbled at his lower lip, then stroked it with one long, slow pass of her tongue.

"Tiffany!" he warned. "If my eyes get any greener, we're both in trouble."

One hand slid up over her ribs until it touched the first full curve of her breast. Warm fingers closed over the soft, resilient flesh, caressing it in subtle, evocative gestures that made Tiffany breathe fast with excitement.

His green eyes holding Tiffany's with the magnet of love, Kirk put his finger in her mouth. He passed it over her teeth and let it play with her tongue. Then he drew it along her pouting lips, moistening them for his kiss.

Her lips and mouth now tingled with arousal, and Kirk's kisses thrilled Tiffany more than ever. She swayed toward him, giving herself over to his long, skillful hands that slowly swept the length of her, making promises to every yearning part of her body, promises that she knew he would keep.

Then he started to undress her, removing each garment in lingering motion, kissing each area of smoothly taut skin he took it from. When only the rosy glow of the lamp clothed her and she quivered with the excitement he had aroused, he moved his hand over her, down her arm to the curve of her breast, soothing her so she could wait.

.

He took his own clothes off in a matter of seconds. Tiffany stared at his thoroughly male, muscular form and whispered, "You're beautiful!"

"Beauty is as beauty does," Kirk answered with a devilish grin.

He lifted her in his arms and carried her to her own bed. Visible to each other in the soft light, they celebrated their love in passionate, personal union. Separate and loving, each taught the other the mystery of individual and joined being. When they merged, it was in a oneness that transcended identity.

Afterward, cloistered in the blanket of each other's arms, Tiffany and Kirk fell asleep.

Sometime during the night, as Tiffany lay with her head on Kirk's chest, the steady beat of his heart under her ear, she heard a faint meowing from the store, which was where Edgar Allan often slept.

"That's Edgar Allan," she said sleepily.

"Doesn't sound as though he's in any kind of trouble."

"No," she agreed. "He's just talking."

But in the morning, as she poured coffee and put a cup in front of Kirk, Tiffany said, "Remember when we heard Edgar Allan last night and I said he was just talking?"

Kirk fixed her with keen gray eyes. "Uh-huh, I remember."

"Well, it just occurred to me, whom would he be talking to?"

"What makes you think he wasn't just meowing?"

"That wasn't his 'just meowing' voice; that was his talking voice."

"And Edgar Allan doesn't talk to strangers," Kirk said thoughtfully.

Tiffany shivered. "I'd hate to think anyone had been in the store while we were up here."

"I might as well level with you, Tiffany. I've thought for some time that there was some connection between The Red Herring and the burglaries that have been going on. I had the department put a man on, watching the store for a while; but then with the shortage of manpower and a crisis somewhere else, he had to be pulled off. Suppose you tell me something about your employee, Lois Weston. How long have you known her?"

"Almost a year."

"What's she like, personally?"

Tiffany considered. "Intelligent. She reads, knows the stock, and is experienced. A little gossipy, especially with customers. Not too dependable lately. But on the whole, a good employee."

"Love life?"

"I have no idea." Tiffany was surprised by the question. "We never get that personal."

Kirk reached into the inside pocket of his sports jacket and pulled out a slim brown envelope. "Okay, forget Lois for the moment. I brought a couple of mug shots with me." He spread five black and white photos, five by three inches, on the desk. "Recognize any of these guys?"

Tiffany looked at each picture for a long time. She wanted desperately to identify one of the men. If Kirk could catch the cat burglar, at least he would be out of *immediate* danger. But at last, she had to shake her head and say no.

Kirk took all the photos and slipped them back in the envelope and into his pocket again.

"Why did you pick the pictures of those five to show me?" Tiffany questioned.

"Because their MO's—methods of operation—are similar to the ones our cat burglar uses. Human beings are creatures of habit. If on his first attempt a burglar was successful in using a half-inch pry bar on a rear bedroom window, for example, he is likely to continue using the same pry bar or one of similar size."

"I see," Tiffany said meditatively. Then a roguish look came into her sparkling brown eyes. "Are all our mornings-after going to be interrogations and mug shots and hunts for criminals?"

"Sure. You wouldn't want a morning-after that was

less exciting than the night before, would you?"

Tiffany's only answer was a smile. Picking up Kirk's empty coffee mug and her own, she asked, "Will I see you tonight?"

"Will you *ever!*"

"I didn't mean it *that* way."

"Actually, Tom's been after me for the four of us to go out together again. How about tonight?"

"Fine. Invite them here for drinks this time. Sevenish would be good."

"I'll do that and give you a call later on. Make an eight o'clock reservation at any restaurant you think we'd all like."

"I feel married already." Tiffany looked at him with a half-amused, half-rueful expression on her face.

"You are!" His eyes glinting with amusement, he kissed her on the cheek and turned as if to leave.

"Hey!"

Kirk turned back. "Something wrong?" he asked innocently.

"What do *you* think?"

He closed her in his arms then and kissed her long and passionately.

"How's that?"

"Better."

"Now that I *know*." He grinned at her and left.

Tiffany went to the window and waited until Kirk emerged at the side of the house, Edgar Allan beside him. She watched as he bent down and scratched behind the proferred right ear. When he straightened up, he stayed looking down at the cat. And Tiffany guessed that Kirk was wondering, as she had, if someone had been in the store last night, someone the cat knew.

Then the thought went out of her mind as Kirk's quick, efficient stride took him to his car. She put her fingers to her lips and blew him a kiss he couldn't see, a kiss Tiffany intended as a good-luck charm, something to keep him safe. She had tied her life to another man with a dangerous job to do. She had done it deliberately and proudly, and with all the faith in the world that the worst wouldn't happen again.

Chapter 12

TIFFANY DECIDED THE foursome couldn't do better than to return to the Caffé Venezia, the restaurant they had all liked. She called early to reserve a table for eight o'clock, then settled down to the day's work. After her conversation with Kirk, Tiffany found herself paying more attention than usual to Lois and to the people who entered the store. But she didn't see anyone who resembled the men in the mug shots, and Lois remained her businesslike, unremarkable self.

At six o'clock, Tiffany pulled down the illustrated window shades and put the CLOSED sign on the door. She ran upstairs, showered quickly, and changed her clothes. She was putting out coasters and cocktail napkins when Kirk arrived.

He took one step back when he saw her. "Wow! Do we *have* to go out?"

Tiffany smiled with pleasure. She had put on a red jump suit in a clingy material and cut. The suit had a cowl-neck halter that left her back 'and suntanned, smoothly rounded arms bare. A broad black patent-leather belt emphasized her small waist, and high-heeled black pumps gave her the height she wanted.

Putting down the brown paper bag he was carrying, Kirk swooped Tiffany against him and kissed her soundly on the lips. He slipped his free hand down the silky smooth material and let it rest on the rounded curves of her derriere. A tremor of excitement surged through Tiffany. She tucked her body into Kirk's, and let his hand have its way with her.

Kirk held her tight against him. "I wish we could be alone," he sighed. "Later?"

Her head against his broad chest, Tiffany nodded, a happy, deeply contented smile on her face. Kirk stroked her hair, then broke his embrace. He picked up the bottle of wine.

"The Laughlins don't like champagne, so I got their favorite Chianti. I didn't see Tom today," he remarked conversationally on his way to the kitchen. "Are you sure they're coming?"

"I called Gina this morning. She said something cryptic to the effect that nothing would keep them away, but she was getting ready for work so we didn't have time to talk."

Tiffany was looking forward to seeing Gina again. She wanted to watch her friend's expressive eyes and her wide, generous mouth that laughed so easily, as Kirk announced that he and Tiffany were engaged. She was dying to know, too, if a baby was on the way yet.

The refrigerator door opened with a loud click. "What have you got to eat? I've been out in the field all day and I'm starved."

"Hors d'oeuvres, but if you think they won't hold you, I'll make you a sandwich." The doorbell rang. "I'm going to get the door. Rummage around in the refrigerator till you find something you like."

"Suppose I end up eating Edgar Allan's dinner?"

"You could do worse," Tiffany sang out.

As soon as Tiffany opened the door, she knew something was wrong. The usually vivacious Gina was quiet.

Her eyes were puffy from crying, her mouth tight and controlled. Tom, on the other hand, was unnaturally boisterous and hearty.

"Sell you a ticket to the Policeman's Ball, Tiffany?" he said with a big, phony smile.

Tiffany smiled back. "I gave at the bookstore." She glanced anxiously at Gina and at the tense smile her friend was forcing. "Please come in. Kirk's here. He's opening the Chianti and threatening to eat Edgar Allan's dinner."

"That big black cat outside is yours?" Tom asked.

"Yes. His name is Edgar Allan. He thinks his job is to guard the bookstore."

"He's as good as a guard dog," Gina said. "I bent down to pat him, and he hissed and jumped away. For a minute there, I thought he was going to claw me."

"Edgar Allan isn't very friendly with strangers," Tiffany said absently. Her mind went back to the night she had heard the cat "talking." *That* person hadn't been a stranger.

Kirk took care of the wine while Tiffany put a platter of crabmeat triangles and stuffed mushrooms on the round coffee table in front of the couch. When everyone had a glass in hand, Kirk stood in the center of the room, and with his eyes on Tiffany, said, "I've got an announcement to make, friends."

Tom nudged Gina, and for the first time that evening a genuinely happy smile brightened their faces.

"Tiffany and I are going to be married," Kirk continued. His "as soon as possible" was drowned in the duet of excited cries and congratulations from Gina and Tom. For a few minutes, it seemed to Tiffany that everyone was trying to kiss her. Kirk started across the room, Gina took her in her arms for a big hug and a kiss on her cheek, and Tom said positively, *"I* want to kiss the bride-to-be."

The euphoria lasted. Tiffany felt wrapped in the warmth of the Laughlins' affection, especially as Tom seemed as happy as Gina about the news. However, glad as she was that Tom now fully accepted her, Tiffany still felt more comfortable with Gina.

At the Caffé Venezia, the men withdrew into their own private conversation, while Gina and Tiffany discussed plans for the wedding. From time to time, Tiffany glanced at Kirk and Tom. The restaurant was noisy, and Tiffany couldn't hear what they were saying. But it seemed to be a description of a case in the department, a case that involved a shooting.

Gradually, however, things began to come together in Tiffany's mind—Gina's distress and the warning looks she directed at Tom, the men's obvious attempts to keep their voices low, and Tom's nervous boisterousness.

Breaking into the conversation, Tiffany asked, "Who was shot?"

"No one," Kirk said quickly—too quickly, Tiffany thought.

"I want to know," she insisted, quietly but firmly.

Kirk shrugged. "Some creep took a pot shot at Tom last night and missed."

"I caught him," Tom explained to Tiffany. "All he did was singe my hair," he added with a laugh, putting his hand to his head.

"What kind of case was it?" Tiffany asked in a half-whisper. An icy chill pervaded her body. Everything in her wanted to contract and hide.

"Armed robbery of a liquor store. We got him cold. It'll be a long time before he draws a gun again."

"Was anyone hurt?" Her voice seemed to come from far away, from across a bare tundra covered with snow.

Tom hesitated. "The night clerk, but he's expected to pull through."

As Tom continued to describe the incident, Tiffany's eyes flicked again and again to Gina. There was a deadness in her expression Tiffany had never seen before. Once in a while, Gina smiled reassuringly at Tiffany, but there was none of her old gaiety in the smile.

The cavernous, hollow chill Tiffany had felt earlier

spread. It seeped into every pore of her being, every chink of her consciousness. It was fear, made worse by helplessness. She and Gina were passive bystanders, powerless to prevent the wounding or deaths of their men.

Tiffany thought she must have shown what she felt, because soon Gina was giving *her* shrewdly assessing glances.

As soon as Tom finished his account of the armed holdup, Gina said decisively, "I'm going to the powder room. Will you come with me, Tiffany?" The dark-haired woman laughed shortly. "I need help with a broken strap."

Tom raised his eyebrows. "Better go, Tiff. That's the one that holds up the whole works."

The women's room was empty. Gina leaned against a sink and looked straight at Tiffany. "The broken strap was an excuse. I know you're upset by Tom's close escape. I am, too. But the worry will pass. It always does. And then I'll be my old adorable self. In other words, Tiffie, ride with it. Don't let it get you down. Above all, don't let it affect your engagement to Kirk. He loves you very much. It would hurt him badly if he lost you."

Suddenly, Tiffany felt very much alone. She had been mistaken. These weren't *her* friends. They were Kirk's and only Kirk's. She had told Gina about Owen. Why couldn't Gina see that Tom's narrow escape had reawakened Tiffany's terror of having Kirk taken from her, as Owen had been? If Gina were truly her friend, she would be thinking of her as well as of Kirk, and she would understand that Tiffany *had* to reassess her engagement.

Wounded by what she considered Gina's callousness about her feelings, Tiffany answered coldly, "What I do about my engagement is a matter for *me* to decide, Gina."

Gina recoiled as though she had been struck. Tiffany was stabbed by compunction when she saw the hurt look on her friend's face. She put her hand out as though to take the sting out of her words, but Gina moved away before Tiffany could touch her.

Tiffany turned on her heel and walked out. The unhappiness she had just caused seemed microscopic and fleeting compared to the well of misery she had been hurled into.

When Tiffany reached the table, Tom asked, "Where's Gina?"

Tiffany forced a bright smile and said, "Coming." She would finish out the evening as cheerfully as she could. But she didn't look at Kirk. What she planned to do would hurt too much if she had to see the love in his eyes. And Gina avoided her without making a show of it.

When they had finished dinner, Gina claimed fatigue.

"First sign of pregnancy," Tom joked.

Even so, Gina insisted that this time she and Tom be dropped off at the BART station at Market and Powell, and so Tiffany found herself alone in her apartment with Kirk sooner than she expected to be.

"This is great," Kirk said, as he helped Tiffany off with her coat. "Much as I like Gina and Tom, I like being alone with you even better." His hands roamed the soft curves under the clinging jump suit. "I wonder why," he whispered.

Tiffany took his strong hands in hers and placed them firmly at his sides. Then she moved away from him.

Hands clenched into small, tight fists, her head thrown proudly back—she wouldn't take the coward's way out and not look him in the eye—Tiffany said, "I'm breaking our engagement, Kirk."

"After just one day? You're kidding. If you wanted to marry me yesterday, why don't you want to marry me today? Don't tell me, let me guess. I've got bad breath...no insurance...I don't have a smoke alarm in my house."

Tiffany resisted her desire to laugh. She turned her head away. For a moment, she felt that she couldn't look at that handsome, vivid face that had grown so dear to her and do what she had to do.

Then she faced him again and took a deep breath. "I told you about Owen and my living in fear every day that something would happen to him—until finally it did." Her voice dropped and became tremulous with imagining her desolation if she got a fatal phone call about Kirk. "I've thought about it some more, and I've decided that I couldn't go through it again. Not with anybody, but especially not with you."

He went to her then and with one finger under her chin turned her face up to him. "I'll help you deal with your fear, Tiffany. Maybe Owen didn't, and that was part of the problem. It won't be you alone facing up to it; it'll be both of us. Sharing our fear will help me, too."

Tiffany looked full into his eyes. "No, Kirk. You don't understand. I didn't tell you because I didn't even acknowledge it to myself until now; but my fear eroded our marriage—Owen's and mine. I was hurt because he let me suffer when he could have prevented it by changing jobs. I fought against feeling that way, but a residue of resentment always remained. Granted, I was younger then, but I can't honestly say that in time it wouldn't happen again—that I wouldn't feel the same way. Believe me, it's better to break off now while we still can."

A scowl drew Kirk's dark brows together. His eyes became cold and gray and hard. "Obviously, it was Tom's getting shot at that precipitated this decision of yours. Did you notice how well Gina took it? And it was *her* husband, after all, not *yours,* whose life had been jeopardized. This isn't the first time, either. Gina's been a cop's wife for four years. Think of all the other wives and kids out there. If everyone felt like you, there'd be no married cops."

Tiffany had always rebelled against having the feelings and values of other people foisted upon her. Now she flared up. "I wasn't cut out of a cookie mold, Kirk. I don't know how other women handle their fear. Each of them, I suppose, has her own way. Mine is to avoid what I know ahead of time I won't be able to cope with."

The dawning realization that Tiffany really meant to break their engagement showed in Kirk's face. He looked suddenly haggard. His eyes became deep wells of despair, and he went pale under his tan.

Seeing him like that broke Tiffany's heart. She longed to go to him, throw her arms around him, and press her lips to his. But she didn't. He'll get over it and so will I, she told herself. And it's better this way.

Without speaking, he turned away from her and walked to the door. Then he faced her. It was obvious he had mastered his emotions. His face was a polite mask, his voice, cool and controlled. "I'll still be around. I'll have to be till we catch the cat burglar. But don't worry, I won't bother you."

Suddenly, he changed. His eyes snapped with anger; his lips curled in contempt. "I think your so-called fear is just a pretext. Why don't you come right out and say you don't love me? You could at least be honest about it."

The door closed with a click of finality. Tiffany stood looking at it, unable to believe that what she had set in motion had really happened. Loving each other, she and Kirk had nevertheless split up. Had she been right to wrench their lives apart like that? With a sad kind of wisdom, she said yes. She and Kirk would survive their pain. People always did.

Abruptly, Tiffany became aware of Edgar Allan, rubbing against her legs and meowing for attention. She picked the cat up and buried her face in his thick fur. The affectionate contact with another being, even an animal, released the tight control Tiffany had kept over her feelings. She started to cry, softly at first; then, after putting the cat down and throwing herself across her bed, in loud, gasping sobs.

At last, when she could stop and had blown her nose and bathed her eyes, she felt better. She went into the kitchen and opened cans—country chicken cat food for Edgar Allan and chicken soup for herself.

"You can't beat chicken, Edgar Allan," Tiffany said, as, still sniffing, she put his food bowl, inscribed, in French, *Chat,* on the floor. "It nourishes and comes in cans." As the click of her spoon against the soup bowl and the cat's gobbling of his food became the only sounds in the quiet kitchen, Tiffany laughed wryly. "If we're going to spend the rest of our lives eating together, Edgar Allan, I wish you'd do it with less noise."

Tiffany went to bed with a mystery that had just come into the store, but her mind wasn't on the book. She got the detective confused with a man who was killed in the first chapter, and kept losing her place and rereading pages without realizing it.

Her mind was on Kirk's accusation: "You could at least be honest about it." It hurt Tiffany that he would think she had used her fear as a pretext to break the engagement. But if he believed she had split up with him because she didn't love him enough to marry him, so be it. It was results that counted, and a clean break was the only way.

She fell asleep early, grateful for that long, dark slide into oblivion. When the phone by her bed rang, her first impulse was not to answer it. Why wake up to unhappiness before she had to? But the ringing didn't stop. Tiffany thought of her parents and the possibility of an emergency.

But it was Gina, an angry, incoherent, passionately indignant Gina.

"What have you done to him? He's been over here since he left your place, and he's wild, absolutely wild. He said you broke it off because you were *afraid* to be a policeman's wife."

Gina's voice dripped contempt. Tiffany shivered under the impact of it. She thought of hanging up. But she understood how Gina felt, and her liking for the other woman kept her listening.

"I couldn't believe it. I still can't believe it. Tom says he's not surprised, but I know you better, Tiffany. How

could you do this to Kirk? You would get used to his
being in danger. I did, with Tom. Everyone does. Or
wasn't that the real reason?"

Tiffany didn't answer. Again, an awful feeling of
aloneness gripped her. Nobody even tried to understand
how she felt, and in a mood of stubborn defiance, she
refused to explain herself any further. She felt sick and
confused and hurt. On top of the terrible pain she had
inflicted on herself by giving Kirk up—and the guilt of
having hurt him, too—there was this attack on her mo-
tives. It was allowable in Kirk. He had been hurt. But
did she have to take it from Gina and Tom?

Tiffany replaced the receiver quietly. She slid back
under the covers and, finally, in the first gray light of
dawn, fell asleep again.

Chapter **13**

THE NEXT DAY, Tiffany got down to the bookstore early and took a long, sharp look around. The store had been her life until she'd met Kirk. Now she had the feeling that she hadn't even been there for days, so absorbed had she been in Kirk.

An old notice about a meeting of the Followers of the Red Herring still hung on the bulletin board. A number of paperback authors were out of alphabetical order. And here it was October and she hadn't even chosen the books for the Halloween window display or done anything about store decorations.

Tiffany didn't blame Lois. There was only so much a person could accomplish in a day. She did, however, blame herself. One could do without love, if necessary, but Tiffany, at least, couldn't do without a livelihood.

She had lost contact with customers, too, she decided. So, when Lois came in, Tiffany turned the routine tasks over to her and got ready to take cash, wrap books, and answer questions.

Late in the afternoon, Pinky Ring walked in, dapperly

dressed as always and carrying the inevitable brown leather portfolio.

Curious about the man's taste in mysteries, Tiffany watched as he methodically moved along the shelves, reading all the titles. Then she gave her attention to Mrs. Rasmussen, a regular customer who was looking for an Agatha Christie she hadn't yet read. As Tiffany patiently went over titles and plots with the woman, she saw Pinky Ring pick a book off a shelf and carry it to Lois.

Tiffany's curiosity quickened. What *did* Pinky Ring read? Excusing herself to Mrs. Rasmussen with a bright smile, she sped to the counter. "Can I help you?" she asked the young man.

She had taken him unawares, and he started and grasped the book defensively. Tiffany looked down to read the title and again noticed the gold ring set with small diamonds.

"That's all right, Tiffany," Lois said in her heavy, mellifluous voice with just a touch of authority in it. "I'll take care of it."

Tiffany answered in a voice even heavier, more mellifluous, and definitely ringing with an I'm-the-boss-here timbre. "You're more of an Agatha Christie fan than I am. Why don't you help Mrs. Rasmussen while I take care of this gentleman."

As Lois toddled off with a bright smile on her face and a worried look in her eyes, Tiffany picked up the paperback that Pinky Ring had laid on the counter. "You're a Simenon fan, I see," she said pleasantly.

"Oh, yeah. He's the greatest." The young man smirked in an arrogant, patronizing way.

Tiffany rang up the sale, put the book in a plastic bag with the store's new logo, a big black cat, on it, and handed the bag to her customer. His eyes held hers for a moment. They were as expressionless as blue buttons. With a brief, dismissive smile, Tiffany turned her back on him and busied herself with the microfiche.

Her heart was pounding. The book Pinky Ring had bought was not one of Georges Simenon's famous Inspector Maigret stories, but detective fiction by another author, a newcomer to the field.

Wasn't there something suspicious about a man who came in as often as Pinky Ring did, bought a book without even a glance at its author, and hung around until he could be waited on by Lois? Should she tell Kirk? Tiffany wondered.

As Pinky Ring walked out of the store, Mrs. Rasmussen came up to the counter, an Agatha Christie in her hand. "I thought I had read *all* of them," she trilled, handing Tiffany a charge card, "but that clever assistant of yours found one I didn't even know existed."

Tiffany smiled politely, but her face was taut with anxiety.

When the store was empty of customers, Lois said, "Tiffany, may I speak to you, please? It's important." Tiffany nodded, her eyes wary. Lois hesitated a moment as though unsure how to go on. "That man ... you've probably noticed he comes in often ... and that he prefers to be waited on by me." A dull red flush bloomed in Lois's sallow cheeks. "Well, he does that because he's ... well ... interested in me."

At first surprised, then relieved, Tiffany laughingly acknowledged Lois's hesitation. "But that's wonderful, Lois! I mean, it's very nice to have an admirer. Do you like him, too?"

Lois Weston was full of surprises that morning. Her face suddenly crumpled and she looked very close to tears. She nodded, then blurted out, "But he's married."

Tiffany caught her breath in sympathy for Lois. Now she understood the reason for Lois's frequent absences and for Pinky Ring's behavior. The couple had to resort to subterfuges to see each other.

But Tiffany also felt a twinge of disappointment. She had started imagining how Kirk's voice would sound and what he would say when she called to report a suspicious character. Still, she told herself, even that pleasure was better foregone. The less contact she had with Kirk, the sooner her heart would heal.

But work was the best anodyne, and Tiffany now plunged into activity. She took Kirk's advice and put brighter lights in the store. She rearranged shelves, added displays, and planned a Red Herring Halloween film festival.

Every time she thought of Kirk, Tiffany resolutely pushed him out of her mind. And to pass the time, she accepted Bennett's invitation to play bridge at his mother's house.

Then one day Gina came into the store.

"Can you recommend a good mystery?" she asked with a disarming smile. Tiffany smiled back, but Gina had hurt her too much for the response to have any warmth. "I really came to apologize, Tiffie," Gina said. "I was out of line when I called you last week. I felt so sorry for Kirk, I couldn't see your side of it. And I'm a woman—I should have."

"At least you said what you honestly felt."

"At the time, yes. But I've thought it over, and I came here today to tell you that I don't blame you. I know you went through this fear trauma once—with your husband—and I understand how that could have sensitized you, made you more fearful than you might otherwise be."

"That could be," Tiffany admitted, "but even so . . ." She was about to say that knowing the reason for her feelings didn't make them less valid, when Gina interrupted her.

"Most people think courage is a virtue, but I'm not so sure." Gina looked off into the distance and her voice took on a musing quality. "As an ex-coward, I think you're lucky if you have the courage that life demands at one time or another. When Tom and I were first married, I was practically paralyzed with fear every time he went out in the patrol car. Then, gradually, I got used to it. Oh, I still react, but I'm not ridden by fear the way I used to be."

Tiffany's eyes shone with joy at the understanding Gina was offering her. "But we're all different . . ."

"I know that," Gina interrupted again. "And please don't think I came here to make a pitch for Kirk. I just want you to know that I understand and that frankly I don't think you should marry Kirk, feeling as you do. I think you made the right decision."

"That means a lot to me, Gina," Tiffany said softly. "I value your opinion and your friendship."

Gina smiled. "You've got 'em both. A big heart and a mouth to go with it. Now, how about that mystery? I've got to have something to read while I'm waiting to see my obstetrician. You have no idea how busy he—"

"Gina!" Tiffany screamed. "You're..." Gina waggled her eyebrows up and down and smiled. "When?"

"June."

"What does Tom think?" It was a silly question, but Tiffany couldn't let go of this happy subject.

"He and Kirk went shopping for junior baseball bats. That'll give you some idea of what I'm in for."

"What if the baby's a girl?"

Gina made a face and laughed. "I can *still* be a Little League mother."

"Never mind, Gina," Tiffany half-crooned. "I'll give her organdy party dresses and we'll put ribbons in her hair." Embarrassed then by the picture she had raised of the four of them together again, Tiffany hurriedly said, "Let's pick out the best waiting-room mystery we can find, and this one's on me."

Tiffany thought of Gina again as she went upstairs after the day's work was over. She decided that she would learn to knit or crochet so that she might make something with her own hands for the baby. Even if it was a botched-up pram blanket, at least it would have been made with affection.

In the meanwhile, however, she had the store's books to do. So after supper, Tiffany sat down at the kitchen table with Edgar Allan curled up at her feet and a tape of Mozart horn concerti on the stereo, to post the journals to the ledger.

A quick loud rap at the downstairs door startled her.

Kirk often knocked like that.

"Excuse me, Edgar Allan," she said mechanically, as a diversion to her fast-beating heart.

This time Kirk didn't scold her for opening her door right away. "I'm here on police business, Tiffany," he said immediately, as though afraid she might think he was going to intrude on her. "I'd like to search your basement."

"You're welcome to, of course. But do you mind telling me why?"

"We still haven't found where the loot from this area is being fenced, so there's a good possibility that it's being hid somewhere till it's no longer hot. Your house could be the one the cat burglar is using. It has a basement—the only one in the neighborhood—and because of the bookstore, there's a lot of coming and going."

Tiffany nodded to show she understood. She could hardly stand the pain of being with Kirk, the way he was with her now. It used to be that every time he looked at her, he seemed to reach for her. Now he looked, and his eyes glanced off her as though she were an inanimate object.

The aching need she had to go to him, to touch him and be in his arms, was overwhelming. Fighting it made her feel inert, rooted to the ground, her limbs heavy and lifeless. This sensation was so painful that, needing to say something, she thrust aside her aversion to mice and asked in a dull, flat voice, "Do you want me to come with you?"

"If you want." Kirk's tone was cool, but there was a flicker of eagerness in his eyes.

Her heart pounding at being close to him again, Tiffany led the way down the rickety old steps into the basement. She opened the door and flicked on the light.

The room was a jumble of period furniture. A cheval glass, an overstuffed sofa, a pair of long-stemmed, lily-like Art Nouveau lamps, an oaken coat rack, and a silver soup tureen on top of an old-fashioned trunk were grouped against a wall.

Kirk let out a long, sibilant whistle. "This looks like Queen Victoria's living room."

"This is some of the stuff that was in the original home. My mother took most of it. I suppose she didn't want this." Tiffany looked around her dubiously. "It might have some value, but frankly I think it's ugly." She shrugged. "I guess I just forgot about it. Out of sight, out of mind."

Kirk strode around the room, looking at every item closely. "None of this stuff came from the cat burglar." He moved quickly to the trunk and flung the lid open. "Empty!" He sounded disappointed. Then he rapped his knuckles decisively on its faded canvas. "I'd like to stay in the house for a couple of days, if you don't mind. Don't worry, I won't bother you. I'll sleep down here on that sofa. Just don't tell anyone I'm here. All right?"

"Sure, Kirk. I'm as eager as you are to have the cat burglar caught." Tiffany's voice was strained. She felt a dull, aching hollow inside, where everything vital used to be. He was cold and impersonal—the police managain. Could love die that quickly? Seemingly, it could.

Tiffany wondered if she should tell Kirk about Pinky Ring, then decided not to. Her own suspicions had been eradicated. Why cause unnecessary trouble for someone? Besides, this man with the lean, hard jaw and dispassionate gray eyes did not induce confidences.

"I'll get sheets and blankets for the sofa." Tiffany eyed its curving shape and narrow width doubtfully. "Will you be comfortable there?"

"That doesn't matter," Kirk said brusquely.

"By all means, use the kitchen and help yourself to anything in the refrigerator. I'll make breakfast in the morning." She hated the way she was babbling on and on, but he *was* a guest in a way and these details *had* to be taken care of. "We'll have to share a bath."

"I'm sorry to put you out like this, but I don't think it will be for long."

"You're not putting me out, Kirk." Tiffany kept her

voice as flat and distant as his. "I understand you have to do your duty."

"*Do* you! Well, that's an improvement, isn't it?"

"I never tried to interfere with your doing what you had to, Kirk."

"That's true. You just didn't want to share it."

"Let's not go through that again."

"Okay. We'll go back to playing house detective and hostess. I'll help you get the bedding."

Together, they went to the linen cupboard upstairs. Tiffany piled Kirk's outstretched arms high with sheets, pillows, and blankets. They said good night formally and separated.

Tiffany prepared for bed quickly and, when she had finished, put fresh towels in the bathroom that connected with her bedroom. She heard Kirk later, just as she was falling asleep.

The frustration of having him physically so close and yet so far was a sharp, twisting pain inside her. She fantasized the door opening and Kirk's broad shoulders filling the empty space.

He would slip into her bed and tell her that he loved her. She would feel the firm pressure of his arms around her, hear his laugh as she complained about the short, curly hairs on his chest tickling her sensitive nipples, and then she would joyfully yield herself to his lips as his kisses mapped the landscape of her body.

The other door to the bathroom closed softly. She heard his light, quick steps on the stairs, and the opening and closing of the basement door. Her dream of love hadn't lasted long.

Sometime during the night, out on the bay, the mournful bleat of foghorns began. Tiffany woke up to a city swathed in white. Street sounds were faint and muted. There was an eerie feeling of isolation, of being marooned on a ghostly island.

A surprisingly spruce Kirk faced Tiffany across the breakfast table. Rubbing his smooth cheek, he answered her unspoken question. "I always carry the necessities with me, just in case." He waved his coffee cup toward the window and the white cotton that pressed against it. "Thick, isn't it?"

"I like it. It's spooky and Sherlock Holmesy and mysterious."

"It's great in books, but how about driving, flying, and the ever-rising crime rate?"

Tiffany shrugged. "You can't have everything."

"You don't say," Kirk said dryly. He put his coffee cup down and stood up. "Thanks for breakfast. I'm going down to the basement where I belong." He hesitated at the door. "You know those African art objects you have? Maybe I should take them with me, just in case our cat burglar gets in somehow and wants them."

"Oh, I don't think that will happen."

"It's up to you," Kirk said coldly.

The day passed slowly. The people who wished to buy a mystery to curl up with on a foggy day were outnumbered by those who didn't want to go out in the fog. So Tiffany sent Lois home early and, between customers, worked on the *The Red Herring Reader*.

At six o'clock, she pulled down the shades and put the CLOSED sign on the door. Then she went upstairs and started to prepare supper for herself and Kirk. She hadn't seen him all day, but she had thought of no one else. Disturbing memories of the promise in his eyes as they turned a brilliant green and of his bare muscular body as it fulfilled that promise played constantly on her mind's screen.

Now, as she set the table in the dining alcove with a fresh blue and white checked tablecloth, then peered in at the lasagna browning in the oven, Tiffany thought of Kirk in a different way. This was what one did for a husband.

Had she made a mistake in breaking her engagement to Kirk? Wasn't this what happiness was? Being together all the time, forging a relationship as strong and fine as glass out of the crucible of mundane living—the good times and the bad, the fun times and the boring ones, the love and the occasional hate of a marriage?

Yes, that was happiness. And you were lucky if you could have it. If your fear-struck heart didn't lurch crazily inside you every time the telephone rang. If you didn't wonder each time you said good-bye to him if it would be the last good-bye. If, as a result, the worm of resentment didn't come, in time, to lie curled inside love's rose. If, in short, you were married to a shoe clerk or a lawyer or an accountant, but not a cop. Or if you hadn't already lost one husband and, therefore, become sensitized to fear, as Gina had put it.

Tiffany opened the oven door for another peek at the now-bubbling casserole, then slammed the door shut. No, she hadn't made a mistake when she'd broken off with Kirk. As Bennett Powell would say, "Once burned, twice shy." She was unhappy now and so was Kirk. But it would pass—faster now than if they married.

"Smells good," Kirk said, suddenly behind her. "Nice to come home to after a hard day in the basement."

"Did you find anything?"

Kirk shook his head. "I won't waste another night on it, after tonight. Our cat burglar's a clever one, whoever he is. He probably has an ego to match," he added absently, surveying the table. "That kind usually does." He reached for a thick white candle that Tiffany always kept in a brass sconce on the kitchen counter. "Your table looks nice. A candle would be good, too. do you mind?"

"Not at all," she replied with matching formality.

Kirk lit the candle and placed it in the center of the table. Then he turned out the lights in the little dining room.

Tiffany had been in Amsterdam once, on a Student Eurailpass trek through Europe. Suddenly, the room took on the exotic ambience of a café by the canals in the center of the city, where, looking in through the window, she had seen the dark room lit by the glow from a dozen

or so stubby white candles, one on each table, like a
Dutch genre painting.

Tiffany breathed deeply. She could almost smell the
dampness of the canals and the rich odor of good cooking
wafted from the houseboats, colorful with window boxes
of petunias and geraniums.

The lasagna! It was the hearty aroma of Gina's recipe, not Rolpens met Rodekool, that she smelled. Tiffany whirled around to the oven.

"I took it out while you were daydreaming," Kirk
smiled, and Tiffany noted that the candlelight threw his
features into relief. It accentuated the bones of his face,
making him look—not less handsome, but mysterious
somehow. It was too dark to see the color of his eyes.
And Tiffany was struck by the feeling that here was a
man she didn't know.

Kirk held her chair out. As Tiffany sat down, he trailed
his fingers across the semicircle of bare skin above her
crocheted top. He pushed the chair into the table and his
hand hesitated on the crocheted button in back.

Tiffany stiffened, galvanized into heart-stopping suspense. She felt for a second as though she would promise
anything just to have him make love to her again.

At the same time, she knew that if she went to bed
with Kirk now, the die would be cast. She would have
to say yes to his marriage proposal. She couldn't mess
up her life with a love affair of fits and starts, of on-
again, off-again encounters.

Kirk sat down and his eyes studied her over the brown
earthenware casserole. "What are you thinking of?"

Tiffany decided to be candid. "That you might be
trying to seduce me."

A broad smile creased his face. "And?"

"That if I let myself be seduced, I will have crossed
my Rubicon."

Kirk turned to a pair of green eyes shining in the dark,
on top of the stepstool. "Did you hear that, Edgar Allan?
I must be the only guy in California whose girl quotes

Julius Caesar before a big romantic scene." He put a forkful of lasagna in his mouth. "This is good! Did you make it?"

"No, I had it flown in from Rome for the occasion."

"All right," he growled. "Let's go back to square one. You figure if we go to bed together, you'll have to make an honest man of me and marry me. Right?"

"The alternative is a messy affair. We don't want that, do we, Kirk?"

Kirk grinned. "Oh, I don't know. How messy?"

"That's not funny."

"Sorry. But to continue, you can't go to bed with me because you'd have to marry me, but you can't marry me because I have a dangerous job. Do I have it right?"

"Pretty much," Tiffany mumbled over a mouth full of lasagna. It *was* good! She'd have to remember to tell Gina.

Kirk laid down his fork and stared into the candle flame. "Hmm, I wonder what Harriet Vane would have done."

"Harriet Vane had an affair before she met Lord Peter Wimsey and it landed her in the dock, accused of the murder of her lover."

"Then what it boils down to is that you're in danger whether we have an affair or marry. Which do you choose?"

"That's like asking someone you arrest if he wants to be handcuffed or tied up."

"No shop talk, please." Kirk leaned forward and took her hand in his. "I appreciate everything you've done for me—letting me stay in your basement, cooking a delicious supper, satisfying my every want." His eyes sparkling with mischief, he bent forward to plant a kiss in the palm of her hand, but Tiffany snatched her hand away.

"If your every want is a cup of coffee, it's about to be satisfied." Tiffany started to get up at the same time that a furry black King Kong paw landed on her shoulder and became entangled in her crocheted top.

"Oh, no, Edgar Allan! I wish you'd keep your paws off me." Tiffany sank back onto the chair and worked at extricating the cat's claws from the delicate stitches.

Kirk laughed, a deep, booming sound in the quiet kitchen. "Funny, women are always saying that to *me*." He got up and came around to Tiffany. "Can I help?"

Standing behind her, he deftly freed Edgar Allan's claws. Then he slipped his fingers beneath the loose weave of her sweater and with both hands dropped the knit down to her waist. He had just touched his lips to her smooth shoulder when Edgar Allan launched a lightning attack and batted him on the head with his paw.

"Hey, Edgar Allan, give a guy a break, will you?" Kirk picked the big black cat up in his arms and placed him firmly on the floor. "That cat's vicious; you know that, Tiffany?"

"Edgar Allan's very sensitive," she answered smugly, standing and pulling the sweater up again. "He's gone off to brood."

"Well, I'm not going to make up with him. He spoiled what was going to be a damn good kiss," Kirk grumbled. "Want me to help with the dishes?"

"You'll have to turn on the lights."

"Do you really want me to?" Kirk said seductively. In one long step, he came up to her and nuzzled the soft angle between her neck and her shoulder. "You smell so good," he murmured.

Tiffany stepped smartly away. "It's awfully dark for doing dishes."

"You're so right!" But instead of flicking on the wall light switch, Kirk rummaged through a kitchen drawer and pulled out a package of white candles.

"How did you know I keep them there?" Tiffany watched him light each candle, let the wax drip onto a plate, then firmly implant the candle in the still-warm wax.

"Nero Wolfe has nothing on me. I saw them when

you opened the drawer to take some silverware out."

Kirk placed the saucers holding the candles on every possible surface in the kitchen. The flames lit the room with a warm dancing glow and threw huge, flickering shadows on the walls. The ambience was one of gaiety, of celebration, of the impromptu.

"Very nice," Tiffany said, and threw Kirk a dish towel. "I wash, you wipe."

"Aye, aye, ma'am." Kirk saluted.

Next, Tiffany reached for a large butcher's apron that went over the head and tied in back. The front was printed with recipes in black and white newsprint.

Kirk started to read the recipes aloud. Reciting the recipe for ground beef with onions and herbs, beginning with "cook the onions slowly," his gaze traveled across her breasts, down her stomach, and over her hips and thighs.

His seductive, caressing glance electrified Tiffany. Annoyed with both Kirk and herself, she snapped out, "Slow reader, aren't you?" and turned her back. But as she attacked the dishes with detergent and dishcloth, the subliminal image of his answering grin remained with her.

Edgar Allan chose that moment to stalk back into the room and meow a hello.

"Scat, cat!" Kirk said. "We're busy."

Edgar Allan meowed back at him.

"What does he want?" Kirk asked.

"Nothing," Tiffany said sweetly. "Just a little conversation."

"Evidently, I'm not getting anywhere with you, but I'm a big hit with your cat."

"*C'est la vie.*"

"Not my *vie*, it isn't."

He came up behind her where she stood at the sink and put his arms around her waist. Tiffany turned abruptly and saying, "No, Kirk!" splashed soapy water at him. Some of the soap got on his face. Tiffany burst out laughing. "You look like a mad dog, foaming at the mouth."

"You're making me *feel* like a mad dog." Kirk's encircling hands tightened their grip. He held her away from the sink so that she wouldn't be hurt, and brought his lips down to hers in a kiss that sent a trail of iridescent bubbles floating upward to the ceiling.

Kirk and Tiffany separated and stared, astonished, at the kitchen rainbow they had created.

Then they laughed. Kirk wiped his mouth with the back of his hand. And while Tiffany's head was thrown back and her mouth partly open, Kirk covered her mouth with his in a sweet-tasting kiss, filling the enticing hollow she opened to him with his warm breath and the smooth velvet of his tongue.

Both his hands went under her sweater, gentle and warm and heavy. Tiffany arched her back against the sink, inviting his caress. His long, supple fingers stroked her soft breasts, and when the pink nubs hardened between his thumb and forefinger, he breathed a hoarse sigh of infinite satisfaction.

She put her arms around his neck and he raised her with his own two firm hands, lifting her forward and upward, till she felt the strength of his arousal. Desire rose and flowed through her like a dark subterranean river, surfacing here and there when he touched her with his hands or his mouth or body.

"Where?" he whispered. "The kitchen sink, my horsehair sofa, or your bed?"

Tiffany laughed. "You and your choices!"

A pang of dismay struck her. You're crossing the Rubicon, she told herself. There'll be no turning back afterward.

There is no afterward, she told herself. There is this moment, and only this moment. He is all I want.

Chapter 14

"WHO'S MINDING THE basement?" Tiffany whispered somewhere in the direction of Kirk's jaw. It was delicious to be standing close to him, his arms tucked around her, while the fog horns bleated mournfully in the distance and the fog whitened her bedroom window. They had marveled at its thickness—as impenetrable as a window shade and perfect for undressing, when they got around to it. Right now, however, Tiffany wanted to savor every moment, and she knew instinctively that Kirk felt the same way.

As though his hunger for her could never be satisfied, he dropped a shower of kisses on her brow and her sloping cheekbone and the tip of her nose before answering. "I put Edgar Allan down there. He'd frighten anyone off."

"You're not derelicting your duty, are you? I just made that verb up."

"Not at all," Kirk answered smoothly, undoing the button on her sweater. "I made Edgar Allan my deputy." He slid his hands along her shoulders and under the loose weave of the sweater, pulling it down till it fell in rippling folds around her waist.

Ardently, he plunged both hands inside her bra and lifted her lush breasts out. Then he unhooked her bra and tossed it aside.

Her breasts gleamed with their own rosy life in the dull white light of the fog.

"Tiffany!" he breathed, giving vent in one word to all the pent-up longing within him.

There was reverence in his eyes as he looked at her, and hunger in their green depths. A thrill that was a kind of glory raced through Tiffany, and she raised her breasts proudly to him.

He buried his face in the valley between, and the roughness of his cheek against the satin-smooth flesh was of a piece with the strength of the hands that held her and the vigor of the male arousal against her thighs.

"Oh, lover," she murmured as his lips wove a daisy chain of lingering, moist kisses on her full, thrusting breasts.

But warm as his hands were, and though his kisses were tropically hot, Tiffany shivered in the damp air.

"You're cold, angel." He slipped the sweater up over her again, but his hands didn't stop their sensuous caresses. His fingers reached through the wide stitches and teased each pink nipple till it was taut and tingling with excitement.

She ran her hands up under his turtleneck, smoothing them along his skin, relishing the feel of him under her hands.

"You're smooth and sleek, like a baby seal," she whispered. He made a sharp coughing sound in the silent air. "Seals don't bark like that. They go like this." She executed a two-syllable, back-of-the-throat noise that sent Kirk into gales of laughter.

"How can I make love to a woman who barks like a seal?" he complained.

Tiffany wound her arms around his neck again, and standing on tiptoes pressed her words against his lips. "Consider it a challenge, lover, and try."

And he did. Chuckling, he put one hand around her shoulders and the other under her thighs and scooped her up off the floor. He carried her to her own bed and undressed her, removing each garment with exquisite attention to what lay beneath.

"You're gorgeous, Tiffany. I want to love you from head to toe."

Tiffany laughed. "That's only because I'm not very tall."

But he had already started, burying his face in her hair and kissing the smooth expanse of her high forehead. When he finally finished with tongue-kisses of each rosy toe, he said, "I only wish you were taller."

In an ecstasy of delight, Tiffany replied, "It's my turn now."

"All right. But no cracks about my being a seal."

Tiffany laughed joyously. As she slipped his undershirt off him, she buried her face in the thick brown pelt of his chest. "How about a woolly mastodon?" she said, raising her face.

"They're extinct."

"A grizzly bear?" she asked, fumbling at his belt.

"I'll buy it. Want to spend the winter hibernating with me?"

Tiffany punched him lightly in the stomach. "Hold still. I can't undo your belt."

He put her hands gently but firmly away from him. "Tiffany, at the rate you're going, we'll be a statistic— 'Is There Sex After Social Security?'"

When he lay back beside her, his bare skin warm against hers, he murmured, "My little cat," and kissed her behind the right ear. There was no place he didn't reach with his sweet, giving mouth, no area his lean, sensitive hands didn't touch and stroke and fondle.

For a while, she lay inert, too enraptured to respond. Then a flood of love for him broke over her, and she made her hands and mouth and body bearers of gifts to him, too.

A groan that seemed to be wretched out of his very being broke from him. Lowering himself over her, he put his hands under her hips and raised her toward him. Tiffany felt the awesome leap of his life deep inside her. She cried out with rapture, with disbelief in the wonder of it, and a little with the poignant knowledge that it couldn't last.

Afterward, as she lay curled in his arms, her still-taut nipples brushed by the wiry brown hair on his chest, Tiffany laughed. "See! I obeyed your bumper sticker— I cuddled up to a cop."

He smoothed her hair away from her brow, then kissed her there. "We'll have a good life together, you'll see, Tiffie." He ran his hand gently over her breasts and the flat curve of her stomach. "It's not only this—great as it is—or even just the love we have for each other. It's not being alone anymore, too. You with Edgar Allan and me with Monday-night football. You'll find you won't mind being a cop's wife after all."

Tiffany froze. "A cop's wife?" she repeated.

"What else?" he asked, and Tiffany could tell he was genuinely puzzled.

"Kirk, I'm sorry," Tiffany stammered, her voice breaking with anguish. "It's all my fault. I wanted you so much, I couldn't think straight. I convinced myself that you would get off the force, because I wanted so badly to have it happen."

Kirk took his arms away from her. "I could never be anything but a cop, Tiffany." His voice was firm. And Tiffany knew his eyes were a cool gray again.

"Of course not," she murmured. She felt small and insecure, ashamed of herself for having been such a fool. She had not only given herself a double whammy of disappointment, she had also aroused expectations in Kirk that she couldn't fulfill. She dreaded having to tell him the truth. She could stand *her* disappointment, but she didn't think she could stand seeing his. Finally, however, she mustered up the courage for the painful job.

"I don't want to argue about this, Kirk, but I have to tell you that I can't marry you if you stay on the force. Believe me, this is not emotional blackmail. I no longer even want you to quit. You'd be miserable and in time come to hate me, as I'd be miserable worrying about you all the time. So, basically, we're incompatible, darling. These things happen..."

Tiffany's voice broke. She bent her head before the look in Kirk's eyes. They burned with anger and contempt, and his features were rigid with his effort at control.

Abruptly, Kirk got out of bed, and Tiffany steeled herself to face him as he stood before her in all the pride of his maleness and his stoical acceptance of the end of their love.

"Nothing could stop me from loving you, Tiffany. I think if you were a jailbird, a hooker, an addict, I would still love you. You don't feel the same way about me. No matter how you cut it, that's the way it is." He turned and went to the door. "I'm putting another man on tomorrow. I won't see you again."

In the days that followed, Tiffany got up, washed, and dressed mechanically, waited on customers with a professional smile pasted on her face, and worked with a numbing ferocity that she hoped would bring sleep. It was particularly important, she felt, not to think about Kirk, not to engage in fantasies of what might have been, not to remember.

Perhaps he felt the same way. At any rate, he didn't appear at the store. If, as he said he would, he had assigned a man to watch The Red Herring, Tiffany didn't know it. So firm was her intention not to dwell on Kirk that she didn't even speculate who among the people she saw every day might be the detective. She no longer worried about the cat burglar.

Tiffany was even grateful that Lois was frequently absent from the store. That meant longer hours for Tiffany; a larger dose of the opiate, work.

Late one afternoon when business had been slow and the store was empty, Tiffany realized that she hadn't seen Edgar Allan for several hours. Sometimes she inadvertently locked him in the apartment upstairs, and he scratched at the door, leaving long talon marks on the wood.

Tiffany decided to run upstairs to check. She toyed with the idea of closing the store first—a little early—since the chances of a customer's coming in so late were practically nil. But she found that her habit of closing exactly at six was too strong.

So Tiffany left the store and ran upstairs quickly. She had the door unlocked before she realized that Edgar Allan was neither scratching nor meowing. As she stepped inside, a sound in the living room made her pause. Then she rushed forward. If Edgar Allan had been using the couch as a scratching post again—

Tiffany saw the man first from behind and couldn't quite puzzle him out—a figure in a black wool cap, black sweater, and black gloves. He had the Chi-Wara in his hand and was looking down at it. Then he raised his head and seemed to be surveying the room.

Fear sang through her nerves. She had no doubt now who he was. There was even a kind of inevitability about his presence. The cat burglar had finally come to The Red Herring.

Tiffany turned silently, grateful for the chance to escape, wondering why he hadn't heard her come in. Her heart pounding against her ribs, she moved quickly toward the door.

Then he spoke, his voice muffled by what Tiffany now realized was a black woolen ski mask. "I saw you, toots. Turn around and come back."

Pivoting slowly on her heel, Tiffany looked into the long black barrel of a gun. She stared at it, hypnotized. Things like this happened in books, not in real life—not in *her* life. Then her mouth went dry with fear. Her heart crowded her throat. There was a dull roaring in her ears.

The masked figure waved the Chi-Wara at her. "Where's the other one?"

She stared at him stupidly. How did he know there was another figurine? Paralyzed by fear, she couldn't even remember where it was. Then it came to her. She had taken it downstairs to show Lois, whose mystery novel—Lois had said—revolved around a theft and murder at an art museum.

Tiffany felt suddenly, sharply sick, as though she had been struck in the stomach. Lois Weston, who had worked at her side day after day for almost a year, had set her up for the cat burglar.

The other statuette was still in the stockroom. After showing it to Lois, Tiffany had stuffed the shoe box that held it into the office safe. Then, in her distress over Kirk, she had forgotten to bring it upstairs. But Lois didn't have access to the safe and would have assumed that Tiffany had taken the figurine to her apartment.

Tiffany's fear turned into something else. Anger at her assistant's duplicity and disloyalty rose hot and sour inside her. She'd be damned if she'd give her property away to this thug and Lois. "Which other one?" she asked defiantly.

His eyes, glittering and fearsome in the holes cut in the black wool, gripped hers in a menacing stare.

Tiffany's rage subsided. She had no intention of trading her life for a foot-high piece of primitive art. She was on the verge of telling the cat burglar that the statue he wanted was in a shoe box in a safe in the stockroom, when to her surprise he put the Chi-Wara down and pulled off his left glove.

Still holding the gun on Tiffany, his eyes boring into hers, he reached behind him and ran the ungloved hand over the wall. Tiffany understood what he was doing. Never doubting Lois's honesty, she had casually mentioned that the statue she was showing her was more valuable than the other. The cat burglar figured Tiffany would leave the less valuable one in an accessible place, a not uncommon ploy, and hide the other behind a secret panel. He was using his fingers to feel for irregularities, even a difference in the thickness of paint.

As he moved his hand across the wall, Tiffany stared, fascinated. The gold ring set with diamonds was unmistakable. Pinky Ring was the cat burglar, and Lois was his accomplice.

Suddenly, Tiffany tore her eyes away. If he knew she had recognized the ring, she was in mortal danger.

"It's not here. Where is it?" His voice was a low, dangerous growl.

Tiffany answered tremulously. "Downstairs. In the stockroom." Let him take the statue and get out of here quickly, she silently prayed.

In her dimly lighted living room, the small diamonds sparkled with a deadly allure. Like some murderous magnet, the ring kept drawing her glance.

"Show me," he commanded. He shifted the gun to his ungloved hand and waved it at her. "You go first."

He's not even bothering to hide the ring from me. He doesn't care that I'll be able to identify him, she said to herself. In a moment of stunned insight, Tiffany knew with the finality of death itself that he planned to kill her.

She looked at the phone—she'd never reach it; at the window—it was closed; no one would hear her scream.

He pointed the gun at her again. "Get going."

Obeying him, Tiffany started for the door—slowly, as though she were moving under water, against pounds of pressure, as in a nightmare.

Her life was out of her hands, she thought with wonder. It was up to this criminal whether she lived or died. He could snuff out her life in a second, and she would have no more control over it than Owen had had . . . or Tom, when he was shot at . . . or Kirk . . . or even Gina when her time came to give birth.

Tiffany allowed herself a wry ironic smile. It was

Kirk she had worried about, and here *she* was the one whose life was in jeopardy.

She shut her eyes for a moment as she went down the stairs, and reached out to the banister to steady herself. Life seemed unbearably precious. She would settle for any life at all if she could just escape the gun at her back.

Regrets crowded in on her. Instead of living the life that had been offered her, she had concentrated—first with Owen, then with Kirk—on staving off death. And what good had it done her, Tiffany thought bitterly, when death had come, anyway?

Suddenly, Tiffany was no longer afraid. Accepting the inevitable had calmed her. Her nerves were steady and her thinking clear.

I still have time, she thought. He won't kill me until after I have shown him where the statue is.

They were in the store now. Tiffany glanced at the wall clock. Three minutes to six. If she didn't pull down the shades and put up the CLOSED sign at her habitual time, and *if* one of Kirk's men was outside, she might stand a chance.

But the cat burglar had been well briefed by Lois.

"Put the CLOSED sign out," he ordered, his voice a rasping growl. "And pull down those shades. Start moving. And don't try anything, or you won't live long enough to regret it."

The slow walk from the rear of the store to the window was agonizing. Tiffany racked her brain for a signal she might send outside without being observed by the man watching her behind the long black gun. She was halfway there when the solution struck like a flash of lightning.

Tiffany clenched both hands so Pinky Ring wouldn't notice what she was doing and drove her sharp nails deep into the tender flesh of her right palm. When her fingers glided over a sticky moistness, she closed her eyes a moment in gratitude.

She lowered first one, then the other shade with her left hand. Moving in a straight line along the front of the store, she put her right hand on the piece of cardboard that hung from a cord fastened to the top of the door. Taking her time and ignoring the "Hurry Up" yelled from behind her, Tiffany turned the sign so that OPEN faced inward and CLOSED showed to the street. Then, folding both hands into fists again, she wheeled around and started the slow march back.

Pinky Ring was becoming exasperated with her now. His repeated commands to hurry were accompanied by snarled obscenities. But intent on giving her signal a chance and confident that he wouldn't shoot her until he had the other statuette, Tiffany persisted in moving with ponderous slowness.

The long-barreled, snub-nosed gun waved her impatiently into the stockroom. Sick with dread, she twirled the combination and unlocked the safe. She took the shoe box out and looked down at it. Maybe by some crazy, unlooked-for miracle, the statue wouldn't be there. Then she and Pinky Ring would have to look for it, and she would be reprieved for a while.

Holding her breath with foolish hope, Tiffany removed the cover of the shoe box and folded back the thin layer of cotton on top. She stared down at the polished wooden figure, the innocent messenger of her death.

Her hands trembling, Tiffany gripped the box and waited for the cat burglar's snarled "Hurry Up!" Instead, she heard a clatter as of something metallic hitting the floor. Almost simultaneously, there was a loud grunt, a violent expulsion of air, followed by a strangling noise.

Tiffany dropped the box nervously and whirled around. *Kirk was there*. He had one arm under Pinky Ring's chin, holding his head back. The other hand held a gun. The black revolver lay on the floor.

Guns drawn, two burly uniformed policemen came through the door, filling the small room. They seized Pinky Ring, and one of them clapped a pair of handcuffs on the criminal.

"Take him in," Kirk said to the man with the handcuffs. "I'll be there shortly. You," he barked at the other cop, "search the building. Put the cuffs on anyone you see, particularly a woman about forty, a brunette."

As the cops hustled Pinky Ring out, Kirk went to her. He put his hands on her shoulders and looked with anxiously appraising gray eyes into her face. "Are you all right, Tiffany?"

Hysterical with relief, Tiffany giggled. "My grandmother told me never to trust a man whose eyes were blue...and gray...and...and...green...and purple..." Her voice trailed off.

The next thing Tiffany knew, she was in her own bed. A dim light glowed in the reading lamp next to the armchair. And Gina was there, her fingers flying over the white yarn she held.

"Kirk?" Tiffany asked.

Gina put her crocheting down and came to her immediately. "He'll be back. He had to go down to headquarters. How do you feel, Tiffie?"

"All right. Did I faint?"

Gina nodded.

"Was it shock?"

Gina nodded again, grimly this time. "You don't stand that close to death and not react."

"I know," Tiffany murmured. "I know a lot of things I didn't know before."

"I called your doctor," Gina said. "He prescribed a sedative. I'll get some water and give it to you now."

Tiffany was glad to take the pill Gina brought her and slip back into sleep. When she woke up again, Gina was gone and Kirk was sitting in the armchair.

"You haven't taken up crocheting, have you, Kirk?" Tiffany said, in an attempt at a joke.

"Hooked rugs are my specialty." He rose from the chair and sat down on Tiffany's bed. He took one of her hands and raised it gently to his lips. "You've been through a lot."

"It's nothing I'd care to repeat," Tiffany agreed. She closed her eyes and gave herself over to the tide of happiness flowing through her. Then she looked at him, taking note of each crisp, dear feature. "I love you, Kirk," she said slowly, deliberately. "I want to marry you. I want to be a cop's wife. I can't assure your life any more than I can assure my own. I learned that down there in the stockroom." Tiffany laughed softly. "So let's love each other and not think about tomorrow."

She reached out her arms to Kirk and pulled him down to her, resting her cool fingers on his face. He bent his head to hers and united their lips in a long, tender kiss.

When they finally broke apart, Kirk took her hand and put it to his lips again. "I love you so, Tiffany. My life was ashes without you."

Tiffany drew her finger along his firm, straight lips, as though to assure herself once more that he was really there. "Thanks for rescuing me, darling. I'm glad you were around."

Kirk seized her finger and kissed it. "I wouldn't put your safety in anyone else's hands, so I watched your place myself. What I blame myself for is not being there when the cat burglar entered. When I think of what *could* have happened!"

He put his lips to hers in a kiss that simmered with desire. Then he stroked her silky brown hair and pulled the blankets around her, leaving his arm lightly but firmly across her breasts.

With the grin that invariably made her heart flip over and turned her knees to water, he said, "You were pretty smart to think of that trick."

Tiffany glanced down at her blood-smeared hand. "I had to do something he wouldn't notice. The only thing I could think of was obliterating the *D* on the CLOSED sign with blood."

"It worked. As soon as I saw that bloody print, I moved in."

"How did the cat burglar and Lois manage the burglaries?" Tiffany asked.

"It was done very simply. He stole only things small enough to be stuffed into his leather portfolio—cash, jewelry, stamps, small statuary. When he came into the store, he exchanged his bag for Lois's. She either took them home or hid them temporarily in your basement, where you never went because of your fear of mice."

"Do I really have mice?" Tiffany asked anxiously.

Kirk shook his head slowly and grinned. "Not anymore. Not with Edgar Allan around."

"Did I ever?"

Kirk shrugged.

"I wouldn't put it past Lois to have brought some in," Tiffany said wryly. "Why did you change your mind about inspecting the cellar when we discovered it was locked?"

"I decided to let it wait until I had done some more investigating, and I knew I could always come back to it."

"Lois—and maybe Pinky Ring—must have been in the store the night I thought I heard Edgar Allan talking," Tiffany mused aloud.

"It goes without saying that they had keys to all the doors."

Tiffany frowned at the idea of this invasion of her privacy. Then another thought came to her. "Why did Pinky Ring dress the way he did?"

"It suited his ego. Early on, I suspected from his method of operation that he was a conceited wise guy who liked to outwit the police."

"What was the relationship between them, anyway— Lois and the burglar?"

"When he was casing the neighborhood, he spotted Lois as a possible accessory. She was gossipy, knew a lot about the businesses and people in the area, and, as an older, not too-attractive woman, was vulnerable to being courted."

"That's why she took so much time off."

"Right. They couldn't always be together nights."

"Because he was busy robbing houses." A chill went

through Tiffany. "Would he really have killed me?"

Kirk nodded, his face very grave. "He would probably have knocked you out and made it look as though you broke your neck on the cellar steps. Lois wanted the bookstore. She planned to buy it—cheap—from your folks."

Any pity Tiffany might have felt for Lois as a woman so hungry for love that she would commit crimes for it disappeared. Tiffany shuddered, then deliberately wrenched her thoughts away from this morbid subject. She smiled mischievously. "That answers all my questions, Detective Davis."

Kirk's glance drifted to the mystery novels piled high on the table next to the bed. "I guess you'd like to be left alone for a while."

Tiffany, too, looked at the books. She wrinkled up her nose. "Oh, I don't know. Lord Peter Wimsey isn't very sexy. Nero Wolfe is fat. Sherlock Holmes is an addict. I don't like men with grandiose mustaches like Hercule Poirot." Tiffany shrugged. "Inspector Maigret is married, and I never fool around with married men."

Kirk grinned. "Would you consider fooling around with a man who was *going* to be married?"

"That would depend on whom he was marrying. Are you accepting my marriage proposal?"

"What do *you* think!" Kirk grinned, then his face fell. "Don't I get a ring?"

"How about a pair of handcuffs instead?"

"Would you really want me handcuffed?" Kirk said seductively, as he slid his hands down her neck and along her shoulders.

"Maybe not, darling." Tiffany pulled him down on her again. "I can't stand metal next to my bare skin."

He buried his face in the curve between her neck and her shoulder, then trailed his mouth over her warm skin, blanketing her with voluptuous kisses that finished with a sensuous caress of her slim feet. Tiffany's heart pounded with a sweet, piercing excitement. Her blood raced wildly and wonderfully in her veins. She stretched languorously, and looked up into the amorous emerald eyes of the man above her. He smiled lovingly at her.

Tiffany sighed happily. "Who says a cop's never around when you need him?"

WONDERFUL ROMANCE NEWS:

Do you know about the exciting SECOND CHANCE AT LOVE/TO HAVE AND TO HOLD newsletter? Are you on our *free* mailing list? If reading all about your favorite authors, getting sneak previews of their latest releases, and being filled in on all the latest happenings and events in the romance world sounds good to you, then you'll love our SECOND CHANCE AT LOVE and TO HAVE AND TO HOLD Romance News.

If you'd like to be added to our mailing list, just fill out the coupon below and send it in...and we'll send you your *free* newsletter every three months — hot off the press.

☐ *Yes, I would like to receive your free SECOND CHANCE AT LOVE/TO HAVE AND TO HOLD newsletter.*

Name _____

Address _____

City _____ **State/Zip** _____

Please return this coupon to:

    Berkley Publishing
    200 Madison Avenue, New York, New York 10016
    Att: Rebecca Kaufman

HERE'S WHAT READERS
ARE SAYING ABOUT

Second Chance at Love®

"I think your books are great. I love to read them, as does my family."
—*P. C., Milford, MA**

"Your books are some of the best romances I've read."
—*M. B., Zeeland, MI**

"SECOND CHANCE AT LOVE is my favorite line of romance novels."
—*L. B., Springfield, VA**

"I think SECOND CHANCE AT LOVE books are terrific. I married my 'Second Chance' over 15 years ago. I truly believe love is lovelier the second time around!"
—*P. P., Houston, TX**

"I enjoy your books tremendously."
—*I. S., Bayonne, NJ**

"I love your books and read them all the time. Keep them coming—they're just great."
—*G. L., Brookfield, CT**

"SECOND CHANCE AT LOVE books are definitely the best.!"
—*D. P., Wabash, IN**

*Name and address available upon request

Second Chance at Love®

___ 07803-4 **SURPRISED BY LOVE #187** Jasmine Craig
___ 07804-2 **FLIGHTS OF FANCY #188** Linda Barlow
___ 07805-0 **STARFIRE #189** Lee Williams
___ 07806-9 **MOONLIGHT RHAPSODY #190** Kay Robbins
___ 07807-7 **SPELLBOUND #191** Kate Nevins
___ 07808-5 **LOVE THY NEIGHBOR #192** Frances Davies
___ 07809-3 **LADY WITH A PAST #193** Elissa Curry
___ 07810-7 **TOUCHED BY LIGHTNING #194** Helen Carter
___ 07811-5 **NIGHT FLAME #195** Sarah Crewe
___ 07812-3 **SOMETIMES A LADY #196** Jocelyn Day
___ 07813-1 **COUNTRY PLEASURES #197** Lauren Fox
___ 07814-X **TOO CLOSE FOR COMFORT #198** Liz Grady
___ 07815-8 **KISSES INCOGNITO #199** Christa Merlin
___ 07816-6 **HEAD OVER HEELS #200** Nicola Andrews
___ 07817-4 **BRIEF ENCHANTMENT #201** Susanna Collins
___ 07818-2 **INTO THE WHIRLWIND #202** Laurel Blake
___ 07819-0 **HEAVEN ON EARTH #203** Mary Haskell
___ 07820-4 **BELOVED ADVERSARY #204** Thea Frederick
___ 07821-2 **SEASWEPT #205** Maureen Norris
___ 07822-0 **WANTON WAYS #206** Katherine Granger
___ 07823-9 **A TEMPTING MAGIC #207** Judith Yates
___ 07956-1 **HEART IN HIDING #208** Francine Rivers
___ 07957-X **DREAMS OF GOLD AND AMBER #209** Robin Lynn
___ 07958-8 **TOUCH OF MOONLIGHT #210** Liz Grady
___ 07959-6 **ONE MORE TOMORROW #211** Aimée Duvall
___ 07960-X **SILKEN LONGINGS #212** Sharon Francis
___ 07961-8 **BLACK LACE AND PEARLS #213** Elissa Curry
___ 08070-5 **SWEET SPLENDOR #214** Diana Mars
___ 08071-3 **BREAKFAST WITH TIFFANY #215** Kate Nevins
___ 08072-1 **PILLOW TALK #216** Lee Williams
___ 08073-X **WINNING WAYS #217** Christina Dair
___ 08074-8 **RULES OF THE GAME #218** Nicola Andrews
___ 08075-6 **ENCORE #219** Carole Buck

All of the above titles are $1.95
Prices may be slightly higher in Canada.

Available at your local bookstore or return this form to:

SECOND CHANCE AT LOVE
Book Mailing Service
P.O. Box 690, Rockville Centre, NY 11571

Please send me the titles checked above. I enclose _____ Include 75¢ for postage and handling if one book is ordered; 25¢ per book for two or more not to exceed $1.75. California, Illinois, New York and Tennessee residents please add sales tax.

NAME_____

ADDRESS_____

CITY_____ STATE/ZIP_____

(allow six weeks for delivery)   **SK-41b**